THE LOST GALUMPUS

THE LOST CALUMPUS

by
Joseph Helgerson

Illustrated by
Udayana Lugo

CLARION BOOKS
An Imprint of HarperCollinsPublishers

Clarion Books is an imprint of HarperCollins Publishers.
The Lost Galumpus
Text copyright © 2023 by Joseph Helgerson
Illustrations copyright © 2023 by Udayana Lugo

ISBN 978-0-35-841522-0

The artist used gouache, water soluble crayons, pencils and digital
tools (Procreate) to create the illustrations for this book.
Typography by Whitney Leader-Picone

22 23 24 25 26 LBC 5 4 3 2 1

First Edition

For Maggie, Jake, Helen Kay, and the alligator

Acknowledgments: Thanks to the following people for aiding and abetting in the telling of this story:

Kate O'Sullivan, Whitney Leader-Picone, Heather Tamarkin, Udayana Lugo, Greg Schaffner, George Rabasa, Janet Hayman, Dick Emanuel, Dan Rein, Brenna Busse, Eric Altenberg, and the always helpful staff at the Eloise Butler Wildflower Garden.

Chapter 1

Mayor Crawdaddy

Getting Mayor Crawdaddy out of his oak tree usually took a catastrophe. Sometimes two. He was a raccoon who liked his comforts.

"We're being invaded!" I called out, stretching things a bit on account of the snowstorm I was standing in. Possum fur isn't as warm as it could be, especially after dark.

It'd been snowing since sundown yesterday. At first

the flakes had swirled around nice and lazy, pretty as apple blossoms. But soon the snow was tumbling down in earnest, hushing the nearby freeway except when snowplows rumbled past. By midnight everything had been all whited up. Daybreak saw tree branches bowing. When night returned again, the stuff was still coming down, silent and steady, without end, promising to bury the world.

"Who's after us this time?" the mayor grumbled, without sticking a single whisker out of his hole.

So maybe I'd used *that* catastrophe a time or two before. Being his assistant meant dreaming up so many of them that I'd sort of lost track.

"Nobody knows what he is," I answered.

"*He?* You mean we're only being invaded by one of them?"

"So far," I admitted. "But he's a big one."

"Some are," the mayor said, turning awful philosophical. He had a tendency to get that way when duty called—it bought him time to dream up excuses.

"Not like this one," I promised.

"All right, Gilligan," he grumbled, "I'll bite. How big is he?"

"Bigger than anyone in the park."

"Even the bucks?" He wasn't buying it.

"Easy. And he's over in the bog, along with everyone else."

I added that last bit to get him moving. Hearing that everyone had gathered without him had been known to light a fire under the mayor.

"If you think I'm traipsing all the way over there in some blizzard—" he lectured.

The bog wasn't that far away, just across the road and over a hill.

"Say," the mayor declared, interrupting himself as if inspired, "are you sure this isn't some kind of mirage or anything of that sort?"

Often as I'd resorted to catastrophes to get the mayor moving? He'd counterattacked by suggesting I was imagining things. Staying dry and warm and comfy was always high on the mayor's list of important things to do.

"If it's a mirage," I said, "it's the first one I've ever heard of that liked to munch on twigs."

"Twigs?" He snorted. "What are we dealing with? Some kind of oversized beaver?"

"Not that I know of."

"Gilly, Gilly, Gilly," he moaned at me all woeful-like, as if I was the sorriest excuse for an assistant he'd ever had. "Have you been suffering from those fainting spells again?"

Pinning it all on me pleased Mayor Crawdaddy no end. But just because I was a possum and had been known to play dead from time to time, and might have had a vision or two while doing it, that didn't mean he had to go blaming me for having to leave his nice, cozy den. Well, two could play that game. I decided it was time to throw another log on the fire.

You see, I wasn't the mayor's only assistant. He kept me around to do all the legwork, and take the blame, and because the votes of all my brothers and sisters and cousins came in handy whenever there was an election. His other assistant was the Earl of Sussex, a runty red squirrel who didn't know anything about Sussex except that it sounded grand when tacked on to the end of the name his mother had given him. He had himself some big plans, Earl did. Better make that BIG PLANS, as in someday being mayor himself. Crawdaddy made him an assistant so's he could keep an eye on him.

"Your Honorableness," I said, knowing how much he liked to be called that, "I guess you could just let Sussex handle it."

Right away the mayor's masked face popped out of his hole. "What's he doing over there?"

"Talking," I said, though I hardly needed to mention that. When wasn't the Earl of Sussex gabbing away?

"To?"

"Anyone who'll listen. Several who won't."

That did the trick. Imagining Sussex steal his spotlight was too much to bear. The mayor flopped his roly-poly self out of his den and waved for me to lead the way. He wasn't about to go plowing through any snowbanks first. That was my job.

Not a single word got said about how pretty the woods looked that night in the fresh jumble of snow. The lights from the city surrounding our park made the sky so glowy and deep that it was awfully hard to keep from stopping to gaze up in wonder. That wasn't all that was going on up above, either. Lightning kept flashing and scraping the cloud tops, splashing pinks and even some greens around. So far as I knew, lightning was supposed to be a summer thing. Seeing it during a blizzard took my breath away. Hearing the thunder that went with it left me pondering what else this storm might have tucked away inside it.

We kept moving, though. Once Mayor Crawdaddy started worrying about what the Earl of Sussex was up to, nothing short of a tidal wave or volcano could stop him. And we didn't get those kinds of natural disasters around here—only tornadoes, hailstorms, and blizzards.

Chapter 2

A Meeting in the Bog

We all lived in Theodore Wirth Park, which we wouldn't trade for anywhere else. It's a big old hilly spread with hundreds and hundreds of acres that are surrounded by the Twin Cities of Minneapolis and St. Paul.

Our home's stocked with woods and prairies, lakes and marshes, and one small quaking bog, which was where we were being invaded. Rumor had it that the bog was the oldest corner of the park—it was always a little colder, a little stiller there than anywhere else. The plants there were different, too, as if they'd been hanging on for ages while the rest of the world passed them by. Tucked away in a shallow valley, the bog was home to spongy ground cover, bare tamarack trees, and marsh marigolds that were all being buried beneath the falling snow. It felt like a forgotten place in a forgotten land. We liked it that way. When you're surrounded by millions of people, being overlooked isn't a bad thing. It improves your chances of survival.

There's a small pond at the bog whose water stayed black no matter how many snowflakes tried to fill it. With winter just getting started, it wasn't even iced over yet. All the animals gathered near the pond that night were gawking and sniffing and tilting their ears toward our uninvited guest.

The four-legged beast before us returned the favor, seeming a bit dimwitted or addled. He stood there munching on twigs and slowly shifting his large dark eyes from one of us to another. Hard as he studied each of us, I got the idea that he didn't believe what he was seeing. Either his eyes were weak as a mole's, or else

squirrels and rabbits and blue jays and foxes and deer and woodpeckers and so on were unheard of where he came from.

A foot taller than the park's biggest buck, and way thicker, he just stood there, letting the snow pile up on the shaggy brownish fur covering his head and shoulders and back. He belched. Steam rose from his mouth as if there were a furnace roaring inside him. I guess that's what the twigs were feeding. Largish as he was, and quietish as we all were, it wasn't any problem hearing his stomach gurgle and groan as he shoveled down sticks and moss.

And everyone kept an eye on the swordlike teeth curving out of his mouth. There were two of them, both longer than me.

And his nose looked as though someone with muscles of steel had tried to yank it off but failed. What they had done instead was stretch it out fifty or a hundred times longer than before. It flexed around as if searching for someone to grab. The snuffly noises coming from it sounded as though he was suffering from the world's largest common cold. One sneeze from that thing would probably have blown all the mice and voles clear over to Bassett Creek on the far side of the park.

So everyone kept their distance and stayed respectful, even the smart alecks. The standoff lasted until the mayor and I got there. That's when everyone but the beast tried to speak at once.

"About time!"

"Stars and snails, where have you been?"

"We could have all been eaten!" cried the Earl of Sussex, who never missed a chance to let everyone know when the mayor wasn't doing his job.

"Hold on to your tails," crabbed the mayor, who hated being rushed. "Looks to me like we've got him outnumbered." Sitting up on his hind legs, he wiped the snow off his whiskers and masked face for a better look. "Anyone try saying hello?"

"Isn't that your job?" asked Sussex.

"It is," agreed one of the bucks. "And just what kind of nose is that supposed to be?"

"Could be a vacuum cleaner," guessed a flying squirrel.

"That'd mean he needs to be plugged in," pointed out a gray fox named Buffy who liked to stir things up.

"I don't see any cord," said a cottontail.

"Hardly even a tail," contributed another.

"You nincompoops," scoffed a nuthatch named Whoopi. "He's not some human thing. He's an animal, like us."

"I think Whoopi's right about that much," Gus weighed in.

Everyone turned toward the oldest groundhog in the park to hear what else he might say. Gus had spent years studying everything human, along the way picking up loads of words that were news to most of us—*toaster, lawnmower, hockey stick,* and so on.

"I believe that people call those long teeth tusks," Gus went on. "And that nose of his could be something called a trunk. Seems to me there's creatures who have such things."

"What kind of creatures?" asked a gray squirrel.

"I forget," Gus apologized. "It's been a long time since I heard about them."

"Well, he doesn't look like any animal I've ever seen," snorted a buck.

"Who said he could have that cattail?" demanded a

muskrat named Sheldon. He was pointing at a blade of marsh grass dangling from the corner of the creature's mouth.

When you live in a park surrounded by city, resources are at a premium and everyone's a bookkeeper.

"The big galumpus," scolded a jay.

Several birds agreed with that, though no owls. As usual, the owls held back on sharing their thoughts. Not so with an old groundhog named Gigi, who was Gus's younger sister and had a heart twice as big as all outdoors. She had grandmothered half the park at one time or another.

"Say, now," she chided. "Shame on you all. You're scaring the poor thing."

Given his size, that was kind of hard to believe, though Gigi might have had a point. He did look a little trembly.

"All right, all right," Mayor Crawdaddy grumbled. "Everybody settle down."

"Easy for you to say," complained a mole named Cedric who was standing atop a snowdrift. "The brute didn't go stomping on your root cellar with those clodhoppers!

My winter stores got smashed to crumbs! He charged on through as if he'd heard a bugle calling him."

"Who's bugling?" demanded the Earl of Sussex, who didn't like any competition with his chattering.

"Zip it," Mayor Crawdaddy said crossly. "Or there'll be fines."

Of all the reasons he liked being mayor, handing out fines may have been his favorite, though feeling important and indispensable ranked up there, too, but fines usually involved snacks being paid to him—especially crawdads.

"For speaking up?" Sussex cried.

"For slowing us down in an emergency," the mayor answered.

"Highly irregular!" Sussex objected.

"Make a note, Gilly," the mayor instructed me. "Sussex thinks there's something highly irregular about some poor creature seeking shelter in the middle of the worst blizzard in recorded history."

"I never said—" Sussex protested.

"Oh, stuff it, Sussex," grouched Gigi, who was overdue to start hibernating and a little short-tempered.

"An excellent suggestion," agreed the mayor. "Now, has anyone seen the likes of our guest before? It might help if we knew what kind of critter we were dealing with."

Heads turned this way and that as everyone checked in with someone else. Eyes blinked. Noses twitched. Gus scratched behind an ear. But not a one of us had anything to say. Our home had been totally cut off from the outside world for so long that no one had the slightest idea of what kind of animal stood before us.

Chapter 3

A What?

"Could be some kind of moose," said Ozzie, the park's oldest owl.

Of course, nobody believed that. Ozzie just liked to bring up moose every chance he got. He claimed to have seen one when he was young, before he'd settled in Theodore Wirth.

"Or one of them camels," guessed a squinty mole.

"How about an ostrich?" suggested a woodpecker.

"Dinosaur?" asked my third cousin Clifford.

Except for my cousin, and maybe Ozzie, they were all just naming animals they'd heard of but never seen. And Clifford had never seen a real dinosaur, only a model of one that the park department floated in Theodore Wirth Lake some summers.

"Everybody get a grip," the mayor ordered. "We may not know what this rascal is, but we surely know what he isn't, don't we?"

Asking a question that he already knew the answer to always made the mayor's tail all bushy. Usually, one of the turtles or toads or salamanders, one of the cold-blooded, levelheaded sorts, called him on it. But in early November, with snow falling so thick and deep and permanent-like, they were all snug under leaf and mud. In the end a chickadee picked up the slack.

"What isn't it?" the little bird asked. "What? What?"

"Why, he isn't a human," the mayor answered. "I hope we can all see that. And we all know what that means."

"We do?" the chickadee sang out before anyone could shush him.

"It means we're honor bound to help him," the

17

mayor declared, sounding all noble and civic-minded about it.

Mayor Crawdaddy could be awful big on reminding us of the rights and responsibilities that came with living in the park. His comment was met with silence, because we all knew he didn't bring up things like honor and helping out others unless fishing for volunteers. Speaking up now would only seal our fate, for the mayor had a way of twisting most anything we might say to his advantage.

So there we all sat, collecting snow on our heads and eyebrows and whatnots. We were straining to outlast one another, but eventually someone would crack. The mayor? He just crossed his arms and waited us out. The first one to break, well, they would be dangerously close to volunteering themselves for whatever the mayor had in mind.

As for our guest, he went back to munching on twigs and snuffling and watching us all as if he couldn't wait to find out what would happen next.

"Oh, isn't this just like you?" the Earl of Sussex finally cried out, unable to hold his tongue an instant longer.

"Rushing in to help someone who probably doesn't need any help at all."

"Hold on now," the mayor said, turning his reasonable, thoughtful voice loose on us. It was the voice he resorted to whenever conniving to get a job done that he wouldn't touch himself. "Sussex, are you saying that you've had dealings with one of these critters before?"

"Not exactly," Sussex hedged, sensing a trap.

"Well, hang it all," the mayor complained. "How do you know that he doesn't need our help?"

"Does he look like he needs our help?"

Sussex had a point there. Armed with those tusks and that trunk, the beast before us didn't look so helpless.

"To the untrained eye," the mayor allowed, sizing up the newcomer, "maybe not. But, Sussex, how would you feel if you found yourself stranded in a strange woods, surrounded by miles and miles of highways and speeding cars in any direction you cared to turn, and snow coming down so thick you could barely find your tail, if you had one?"

"The poor thing," Gigi said again.

"He looks big enough to take care of himself to me," Sussex stubbornly insisted.

Most everybody nodded yes to that, especially when a really huge lightning bolt lit up the sky and made our ears ring. We all would have rather been home in our dens and thickets and culverts than standing around in a blizzard trying to guess what some stranger was.

"As if size had anything to do with it," the mayor scoffed after the rumbling died away. "But make a note, Gilligan. The Earl of Sussex thinks if you're big, you can take care of yourself. And if you're little, you can't do much of anything for yourself."

Just the way the mayor intended, that squeezed an outcry out of anyone smaller than a fox.

"Now, just a minute," Sussex protested. "I never said—"

"We'll call it reading between the lines," Mayor Crawdaddy blew on, "and leave it at that. But what I really wanted to ask was whether anyone has ever heard any stories from your old ones about what we've got here. You know—myths, legends, family tales. What granny told you when the fireflies came out."

Everyone frowned as if stumped.

"Your honor, sir," a chipmunk finally spoke up, "that beaver who used to come up the creek every spring—he liked to tell stories about something or other he called a horse. Said they were big enough to squash you flat if one of them stepped on you."

We all zeroed in on the newcomer's big, round feet.

"That old scoundrel," squawked Sheldon the muskrat. "I've never met a beaver yet you could believe."

"He sure made it sound real," the chipmunk said. "But I don't recall him ever saying anything about those horses having tusks, so I guess it's nothing."

"As usual," harrumphed Sussex, who didn't get along with chipmunks at all. From time to time he'd been mistaken for one, which he took as a huge insult, for he liked to believe he was twice their size.

"It's a start," the mayor encouraged. "Anybody else have something?"

Our visitor looked just as curious as everyone else to hear what might be said next. There was something real trusting about his eyes. But nobody risked speaking up, not with the mayor still on the prowl for volunteers.

"Gilly," the mayor said to me, "what about that bunch of yours? There must be some possum lore left over from before you reached the park."

"Bears," I blurted with a shiver.

Now, please don't go thinking I shivered because I was scared of bears. Of course I was afraid of them, and most anything else with sharp teeth, especially if I'd never seen them. That was one of the main reasons my family had moved to Theodore Wirth not too long ago. Fewer sharp teeth. Yes, there were fox and coyote and loose dogs in the park, but nowhere near as many of them as there were outside the city. And no bears. Naturally there were plenty of humans bumbling around the park, but none of them were hunters or trappers who liked possum fur or possum pie or possum . . . Well, enough of that.

No, I was shivering because it was winter, that's all. Really.

"But bears are supposed to be big," I said, never having had the pleasure of meeting one.

"This one qualifies there," sang out Sussex.

"Except that I don't recall ever hearing that they ate twigs. Just berries. And those tusks . . ."

"We're rolling," the mayor encouraged, trying to keep us talking. "We're rolling. Anybody else? How about you hawks? You're always bragging about how much you get around."

"Across the river," said a red-tailed hawk from high in one of the bare tamarack trees, "there's that place called a zoo, where humans keep animals behind fences. They've got some real dillies over there."

"Now, that's a possibility," Mayor Crawdaddy enthused. "Maybe he got out of a hole in the fence."

"Must have been an awfully big hole," I pointed out.

"Gilly," the mayor said, all exasperated, "you're always seeing problems, never solutions."

He had me there and didn't I know it. But I never got a chance to deny it. A deep, slow voice that nobody recognized spoke up first.

"What's a fence?"

Chapter 4

A Broken Wisher

It turned out that the big galumpus could speak, though awful slow and bumpy, as if he had trouble calling up more than one word at time. He sure didn't seem used to talking.

"Who raised you?" demanded the Earl of Sussex, making it sound as if they'd done an awfully shoddy job of it. Who didn't know about fences?

The big galumpus pumped a squeaky, sniffling sort of sound out of his extra-long nose and blubbered, "I forget."

Now, that caused a stir. Who forgot who raised them? But as much as the big galumpus outweighed us, and hard as he was scowling at us, nobody rushed to point it out. The only one with anything to say was Sussex, who was safely out of reach in a tree.

"So you tell us. What are you?"

The stranger chewed his twigs a long while before answering, "A camel?"

That got a rise out of everyone and made the galumpus smile as if he'd said something clever. Sussex brought us all back to earth.

"Guess again," the Earl guffawed. "Camels don't have tusks." Before anyone got around to asking if he was sure about that, he tacked on, "Now, look here. Where'd you say you were from?"

"Didn't."

"So where are you from?" the mayor asked when the galumpus got all shy about it.

"Ain't from nowhere," the galumpus answered, awful evasive-like.

"Fiddlesticks!" Sussex sniped. "Everybody's from somewhere. Come on now, where's home?"

The big galumpus gulped and lowered his voice to say, "Gone."

He sounded broken up about it. Shattered, you might say. His answer caused a buzz.

"Gone?" squeaked a bewildered vole named Carmen. "Homes don't just get up and leave, do they?"

The nervous way that vole was looking at the bog all around us? You could tell she was worrying about our home. Quite a few animals were bobbing their heads yes to that question, as if it'd never occurred to them that a home could walk away. It wasn't a thought that was too popular just then.

"Why, that's terrible," Gigi sympathized. "Just terrible."

"Gone where?" Sussex badgered.

But the big galumpus clammed up and shook his head as if he couldn't bear to think of it.

"Breathe," Mayor Crawdaddy urged, taking charge. "Can you at least tell us how you ended up here?"

"Made a wish."

"What kind of a wish?" the mayor asked, intrigued.

He dabbled in wishes himself, usually when facing some chore he'd rather not do.

"The kind you can't take back," the big galumpus said, hanging his head as if he wouldn't mind a do-over. Turning defiant, he added, "But I didn't have anything to do with that cat. You can't blame that on me. He got here on his own."

"Which cat?"

"The one chasing me."

Everyone squirmed uncomfortably at that news, trying to imagine a cat big enough to chase a galumpus. Our befuddlement lasted until a young field mouse named Captain Kirk cried out, "The brute!"

Trust Captain Kirk to take on a cat every time.

"Hold on now," the mayor cautioned. "I'd like to see the kitty-cat who could chase this fellow around."

"A-gosh," the galumpus said, shocked. "You would?"

Right about then was when it dawned on me that no matter how big this galumpus was, he sounded like a kid.

"How old are you?" I asked, catching everyone by surprise.

"Almost five," he boasted, making it sound like a major accomplishment.

"Only almost?" gulped a chipmunk named Opie.

"When you're that old," the big galumpus went on, "they ought to quit treating you like a kid. Don't you think?"

"Who?" Sussex barged in.

"The rest of the herd."

That stirred our tails plenty. Imagining a whole herd of these galumpuses rummaging about Theodore Wirth rattled us good, especially if this one was only a kid. Trying to picture how big he would be when done growing left even the Earl of Sussex speechless.

"What's your name?" I asked, friendly as I could.

"Twigs," he answered, crunching down on a mouthful of the same.

Hoots all around for that. But we sobered up fast when the big galumpus scowled as if trying to wish us all away.

"It's a perfectly good name," Gigi said.

"Well, Twigs," I went on, humbled, "what we were all wondering is, how can we help you get home?"

The mayor nodded in agreement to that, adding, "Wherever it's gotten to."

The big galumpus chewed on that before saying, "Couldn't I maybe just stay here with you?"

Somehow Twigs managed to make his brown eyes even bigger while pleading his case.

"Now, just a root-golly minute," fussed Cedric, the mole whose pantry had been trampled. "This isn't your home."

"No," Twigs reluctantly agreed. "I guess not." Brightening as if he'd had an idea, he added, "But maybe I could make it my home."

"How?" Cedric asked. "You sure weren't born here."

"Were all of you born here?" Twigs asked.

"Pretty much," the mayor said, conveniently forgetting that Ozzie had been hatched and raised in the great Northwoods, and that my own great-grandparents had migrated to the park as northern winters grew milder, and that there were all kinds of migrating finches and warblers who spent time with us but sure weren't born here.

"I see," Twigs said, crushed, though only for a second.

Rallying, he asked, "Does it say somewhere that you have to be born here to make it your home?"

His question started a real hubbub, especially amongst the birds, but in the end, nobody could remember any such rule.

"Hold everything," Mayor Crawdaddy called out, silencing the bog. "Think a minute now. You'd be the only galumpus in the park. How would that ever work out?"

Frowning, Twigs puzzled over that long and hard before meekly asking, "Maybe it could be our secret?"

"We don't like secrets," said the Earl of Sussex.

What rubbish! Sussex couldn't resist secrets. He blabbed them around the park morning, noon, and night.

"Or maybe we could pretend I'm something else?" Twigs suggested, real earnest.

"Like what?" Gigi asked.

"Yeah," several others clamored, wondering what the big galumpus had in mind.

"How about a camel?" Twigs said, trying to jolly us into letting him stay.

But his camel answer wasn't as big a hit the second time around.

"I'm afraid you'd still be the only one," I said, doing my best to let him down easy. "There just aren't any camels in these parts, except maybe on TV."

"Maybe I could join them there."

"Where?"

"On TV."

It didn't sound as if he had any idea what a TV was. He must have been from somewhere far away.

"I'm afraid you wouldn't fit," I said.

"Well, how about one of them?" Twigs asked, pointing his long nose at a nearby chipmunk. "How about if I pretend to be one of them?"

"Don't you think someone might notice that you're kind of big for a chipmunk?" I asked.

"Probably not," Sussex griped, wanting us to remember his troubles with wise guys mistaking him for a chipmunk.

"Maybe we could make him an honorary chipmunk," said Opie, doing his best to be helpful.

"Yeah," Twigs quickly agreed.

"No honoraries," the mayor ruled.

"Well, does having only one of me cause some kind of problem?" the big galumpus wanted to know.

"It sure would," the mayor said. "You'd have people pouring in here from all over to get a look at you. Humans are just crazy for one-of-a-kind things."

"Fair enough," Twigs said. "But what if I wouldn't let them see me?"

"And just how are you going to pull that off?" The mayor snorted. "You sort of stand out."

"I'd make myself invisible," Twigs said.

"How?"

"Same way as I got here," he said, tapping his forehead with the end of his trunk as if there were secret powers locked up inside there. "With a wish."

"Show us," Sussex said, egging the poor galumpus on.

"You asked for it," Twigs warned. Squeezing his eyes shut and puffing out his cheeks, he mumbled something under his breath about a half dozen times. When he finally opened his eyes, he said with satisfaction, "There. All gone."

Bumps on a log didn't have anything on us. We sat

there gaping at the big galumpus as if hoping he really would vanish any second. But nary a hair or tusk of him went missing.

After a half minute or so, we started getting restless and glancing sideways at each other, wondering if anyone else was still seeing him. It appeared we all were. How we were going to break that news to him made us rather uneasy. Gigi finally took charge and spoke up.

"We can still see you."

"Naw," Twigs scoffed, refusing to believe her. "You're just pretending to see me."

"I'm afraid not," I told him.

"From end to end," Sussex smirked, "and everywhere in between."

"My wisher must be all tuckered out," Twigs said defensively, as if he couldn't understand what had gone wrong. "It must have gotten worn down getting me here."

"Let's put that on hold for now," the mayor decided. "Even if you could make yourself invisible, you'd still have an awful lot of trouble fitting in around here. You wouldn't have any idea of what to stay away from."

"I could learn," Twigs promised.

Everyone was starting to slide into uneasy by then.

Living in a park surrounded by people, even one as roomy as Theodore Wirth, didn't give you a lot of extra space. In fact, we didn't have any unclaimed space at all. Everything was spoken for down to the grass patches and dogwood thickets. There'd been a lot of grumbling when we possums first showed up, and some of our neighbors still treated us as if we were just passing through, like songbirds in the spring. And we weren't anywhere near the size of this galumpus, who was still growing. How much would he eat? Where would he bed down? Could he quiet his stomach when humans came around? With questions like that popping off inside everyone's head, we all turned to Mayor Crawdaddy, expecting him to step up and say something intelligent about who got to move into the park. But he wasn't in the mood to talk about park guidelines and scowled at the big galumpus right along with the rest of us.

"What about your ma and pa?" the mayor asked, stalling.

"They wouldn't care if I stayed here," Twigs sniffled, maybe fishing for sympathy.

"Won't they be worrying about you?"

"Not likely," Twigs bawled, breaking down completely.

"There, there," soothed Gigi. "Of course they'll be worrying about you."

"No, they won't. They're gone too."

"Gone where?" The mayor pounced, sounding as if he thought we were finally making progress.

"I'd druther not say." Twigs couldn't bear to think of it.

It was enough to break your heart, unless

you didn't have one. Speaking of, the mayor gave my tail a tug and whispered in my ear.

"Gilly," he said. "A word."

Uh-oh. I knew what was coming: The mayor had something he wanted done, and like most things he wanted done, he didn't plan on doing it himself.

Chapter 5

A Hot Tub, a Trampoline, and Someone to Trust

"Is everyone watching us?" the mayor whispered. He would have been awfully put out if they weren't.

"You know they are."

I could see over the mayor's shoulder just fine, and trust me, every eye was aimed our way, and that included Twigs's large browns. Hadn't the mayor just made a big show of pulling me aside as if he had to tell me something top secret? That meant the Earl of Sussex was having conniptions. Being left out never failed to drive him wild.

"Here's my thinking," the mayor confided. "Try and keep up. There's no way that galumpus over there can stay with us. He might grow to be two or three times bigger than he already is. Maybe more. And he's already bigger than everyone else."

"Didn't I tell you?"

He breezed by that, saying, "He'd eat this park bare."

"It's a possibility."

"And there wouldn't be anywhere to hide him. You know what that means."

"People," I reckoned.

"Lots of people. It wouldn't be much of a life for him."

"Or us," I added, knowing firsthand how the mayor hated having his rest interrupted.

"Or us," he agreed. "I'm thinking that the best thing to do is get him back to his home."

"If we knew where that was," I pointed out.

"That's right," the mayor said agreeably, as if I was making perfect sense. "And I'd say that the first step in doing that is figuring out where his kind belongs. Are you keeping up with me so far?"

"Doing my best."

"I'm thinking we're going to need some outside help to figure out where he came from."

"What kind of help?" I asked, queasing up. It was beginning to feel as though the mayor had a plan, which was never a good thing, not for me.

"The human kind," said the mayor. "They tend to figure things out. If you've ever seen anything like him on those TV shows you're always sneaking off to watch, now'd be the time to bring it up."

He had me there, having caught me more than once or twice watching people's TVs through their windows. I'm sort of drawn to old sitcoms, scary movies, and game shows with flashing lights. The way people in those shows talked was nothing but gibberish to me and every other animal in the park except maybe Gus. Totally meaningless. But not understanding what they were saying didn't stop me from enjoying them. Those TVs spilled the doggondest assortage of sights and sounds you can imagine—flying above clouds, and crawling inside beehives, and listening to whole rooms of people singing together at the top of their lungs.

And don't go thinking that I was the only one in the park who partook of TV shows. There were plenty of others with the habit. Where did you think names like Buffy or Gigi or Ozzie came from? But in all my hours of TV, I'd never run across anyone who looked like Twigs.

"He's news to me," I told him. "And just how are you going to find some human you can trust?" I did my best to pretend that I didn't have the foggiest idea how we'd ever manage that. He played right along with me.

"We'll just have to pick real careful." The old fraud said that with a straight face.

If Theodore Wirth's golden rule was to help your fellow animal, its other golden rule was to stay clear of people. For every one of them who might spread cracked corn or help mend a broken wing, there were two ready to run you over with a car, or swing a golf club at you, or just flat out scream at you as if they'd spotted a three-headed swamp monster—even if you were an itty-bitty garter snake doing your best to dive out of their way.

"And just how are you talking that galumpus into going to see some human?" I asked. "If he's scared of a cat, I mean."

"Gilly," the mayor sorrowed, "you're looking at this entirely backward."

I was afraid he'd say that. And what's more, he'd put a paw on my shoulder all fatherly-like.

"No," I said, on general principle.

When dealing with the mayor, it was generally a good idea to sprinkle "no" around as much as possible, and as soon as possible, just to slow him down a bit. *No* was a word he had trouble recognizing unless he happened to be the one saying it.

"We're not going to take the galumpus to see the human," the mayor chuckled. "We're going to bring the human to see him."

"And just how are we going to make that work?"

It wasn't as if we could walk up to some human and ask them to come take a look at a galumpus we'd found. Even if we managed to find one who didn't start screaming or trying to brain us with a tennis racket, they still wouldn't understand what we were saying. Animal talk was as far beyond them as the gobbledygook they spoke was beyond us.

"Oh, there's ways," the mayor said, scheming.

"No."

"Now, Gilly," he reasoned, "you don't even know where I'm headed with this."

"I don't need to know," I said. "The answer is no."

"Have it your way."

"I aim to," I said, unable to shake a sinking feeling that the mayor was giving in far too easily.

The way the mayor broke out a heavy sigh and wagged his head wearily, as if he had the weight of ten worlds on his shoulders? He was finagling.

"That girl you're so friendly with?" the mayor probed. "She probably wouldn't know where a galumpus like this came from anyway."

The old slyboots. Pretending I was friendly with a girl? There wasn't any end to how low he'd sink to get what he wanted. It wasn't only my reputation he was besmirching with such talk. He was dragging my whole family's name through the gutter, too, and didn't he know it? If someone got to gossiping about my being friendly with a human, cousins I hadn't seen since last summer's fireworks would be tracking me down to ask just what in the seven wonders I thought I was doing, consorting with people.

So I'd like to set the record straight before the mayor grew a little anthill into a mountain. Yes, unlikely as it may sound, I was maybe just the tiniest bit friendly with a girl named Ruth. Her family had a backyard hot tub that could be kind of cozy to crawl under on a cold night. That's how we first crossed paths.

And maybe I had let her snap a picture or two of me hanging from her bird feeder. How was I supposed to stop her while I was upside down? It wasn't like she'd be showing those pictures to anyone I knew.

And when she started calling me Uncle Fester, I told her that I'd just as soon be called Gilly, but being human, she couldn't understand a word I was saying. Gus claimed she probably lifted a name like that from an old TV show.

Pretty soon she'd started sharing a candy bar with me now and then, if I scratched on her window late at night while she was watching TV in her bedroom. Was

I supposed to turn them down? It's not as if it made us best friends or anything. Just friends, although I guess it did kind of point toward some trust between us, a little bit. Or maybe a lot. I'd never run across any anyone else in the park who was on a first-name basis with a human, at least not that they'd admit. And if the mayor hadn't happened across me polishing off a peanut bar one night and wormed the whole story out of me, we wouldn't even be having this miserable conversation.

"Why are we all of a sudden talking about some girl?" I asked, knowing better than to admit to anything.

"Now, Gilly, you and I both know that we've been talking about her all along. She lives just over that way, doesn't she?"

The mayor waved a paw toward the hill on the far side of the bog. You couldn't see it through the falling snow, but that didn't stop everyone else from glancing over that way too. Even the galumpus took a peek. People lived atop that hill.

"Search me," I lied.

"Well, if that's the way you're going to play it," the mayor said, "I guess I'll have to go tackle her myself."

Ha! A big fat HA! Mayor Crawdaddy didn't have any more intention of going after Ruth than the Earl of Sussex had of staying quiet. He was just trying to rope me in was all.

"We'll have to leave you in charge of everything while we go get her," he plowed on.

"Who's we?" I braced myself for the worst.

"Oh, me and Sussex. You wouldn't expect me to go after some human all by myself, now would you? Don't you worry, though. We'll be back before you know it. I'm betting it'll go way better than the last time I left you in charge."

Naturally he had to remind me of that. He and Sussex had gone off to settle some dispute over by the lake beach, and I'd gotten stuck having to rescue one of Gigi's grandkids from a trampoline behind a house that bordered the park. I still have nightmares about it. Me and that little groundhog bounced up and down for what seemed like weeks, shaking up our insides, and scrambling our brains, and screeching for help, and begging for mercy, and promising we wouldn't ever go anywhere near another one of those fiendish contraptions for so long as we lived. And playing dead hadn't been any kind of option either. Seeing me keel over had only made Gigi's grandkid scream all the louder.

His squeals brought a dog running, a hound who raced around us, howling and snapping and finally leaping on the trampoline to tear us to shreds. Luckily, his added weight pitched us off the back side of the thing, and we staggered into the brush before he could come after us.

I still haven't lived that one down.

But what really sealed the deal was the mayor threatening to take the Earl of Sussex with him. He knew full well that both Earl and I would rather wade through a field of stick burrs than be outdone by the other. If Sussex ever did become mayor, I was out of my assistant's job for sure. He'd have me over on the park's golf course, doing sentry duty.

"Mayor," I accused, "you're a sneak, a finagler, and a liar."

"Why, thank you." He flashed me that berry-eating grin of his.

"I don't see what good it's going to do," I said, holding out. "Even if I somehow get her over here, she won't understand a word we're saying."

"So?"

"How are we going to explain to her that we need help getting this Twigs home?"

"Gilly, the trouble with you is that you never quit worrying."

"I thought it was that I was always seeing problems, not solutions."

"That too," the mayor conceded. "Now let me ask you this: Have you ever met a human who didn't think they could fix everything?"

"Maybe not, but what's that—"

The mayor rolled right over my objections, saying, "You get your pal over here and we won't have to tell her anything at all. She'll take one look at this galumpus and see that he needs help getting home. And not only that, but she'll figure that she knows the best way of getting him there too. That's humans for you. And how's she going to know all this? Because one look will tell her that he sure doesn't belong here. And where else would she want to take him but to his home? She sure wouldn't be able to keep him at her house. What would her parents say?"

It didn't take a fox to figure out the flaw in that plan. There were a whole lot of other places where a human might decide it was best for Twigs to go. That place the hawks talked about for starters. The one with all the fences. And the mayor knew it. What was he up to? Trying to wash his paws of the whole business by getting people involved, that's what. I was about to call him on it, too.

Except that just then a flash of lightning pretty near split the quaking bog in half. The thunder that followed it wasn't any chicken scratches either. The rumbling shook everything so hard that it completely cleared my head of doubts and left me with one thought.

I trusted Ruth.

She'd never tried to hurt me or catch me or call a bunch of people to look at the cute possum scratching at her window. No, she'd always treated me like a friend, and when my head cleared, I saw that's what she'd try to do for Twigs, too.

Settling down, I decided to go along with the mayor's plan, though I knew I couldn't just cave in and do what he wanted. If I didn't squawk a little, he'd get suspicious. That's why I pulled a long face and made a counterproposal.

"If I go get the girl, will you make me a promise?"

"You name it, Gilly, and it's as good as yours. You have my word."

Everyone knew that the mayor's word wasn't worth a wormy acorn, if that.

"On your sacred oath as mayor?" I quickly added.

"Now, that's not fair," he said, all resentful.

His sacred oath was the one thing the mayor could be trusted to stay true to. He didn't want word to get around that he'd gone back on that. His position had too many perks that he loved.

"On your oath?" I repeated.

"Done," he grumbled.

"Promise you won't tell Sussex where I'm going," I said. "That's all I ask."

"You know he won't give me a moment's peace once you're gone," the mayor complained bitterly.

"I'm counting on it," I said, trudging off into the snow.

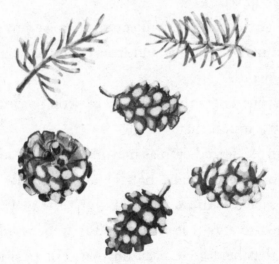

Chapter 6

Uncle Fester

The last I heard from Mayor Crawdaddy? He was doing what he loved best—giving orders.

"Everyone sit tight," he was saying. "Everything's under control."

"Where's Gilly going?" Sussex demanded.

"To get some help," the mayor answered, "unless you'd rather take care of this all by yourself."

"What kind of help?"

"Now, isn't that just like the Earl of Sussex?" the

mayor asked everyone else. "Does someone who's drowning bother to ask who's tossing the lifeline?"

"So now we're drowning?" Earl sassed.

"Doesn't even know when he's in over his head," the mayor continued.

"If you ask me," the Earl of Sussex shot back, "that possum's going in exactly the wrong direction for help. There's nothing over that way but people."

That got everyone to muttering and second-guessing and remembering other errands the mayor had sent me on, errands that hadn't turned out so well. Sussex loved to paint them as disasters. Okay, maybe one of my errands had ended up with a scorched picnic table, but to hear the Earl of Sussex tell it, we were lucky the whole park hadn't burned down. And then there was the time we found that little girl wandering in the woods at night. I got sent to find her parents but came back with a dog. Could I help it if no one else would follow me? But by the time Sussex got through retelling that one, he made it sound as if a whole pack of snarling beasts had nearly ripped everyone to pieces.

"Sussex," Mayor Crawdaddy broke in, "if you've got

some better direction in mind, then I wish you'd speak up. None of us ever get tired of hearing how all-knowing you are, and time's a-wasting. If we don't come up with some answers before this blizzard lifts . . ."

The mayor's voice grew fainter with every step I took, and then it went missing altogether. I stopped and turned around to see if Sussex would try to follow me. Deep as the snow was, I had to stand up on my hind legs to spy over the drifts, and even then all I could make out was the dark, roundish shape of the galumpus named Twigs rising above the bog. Everyone else had been carried off by the blizzard, their voices gone with them.

That was one of those moments that pinch. Here I was, traipsing around in the nastiest bit of weather to blow through Theodore Wirth in years, maybe ever, and who did I have to talk to? Nobody but myself. And right away I found something to say, too.

"Quit stalling," I told myself.

The steepest hillside in the park rose off the back side of the bog, stretching up to a ridge that was lined with people's houses. Ruth lived up there. Even under the best of conditions, scaling that hill left me puffing.

The first snowdrift I waded through was so far over my head that I got lost inside it and nearly didn't make it back out.

The storm kept on raging as if there was nothing but snow between here and the nearest star. And the way the flakes sopped up the sound? The whole world seemed about to go away, never to be heard from again. That only lasted until more thunder and lightning kicked up. The way the air crackled then, I feared that this time the woods really might catch fire and burn down. Every few steps I lifted my nose high to sniff for smoke.

When I reached the hillside, I burrowed upward through all the dumped snow. I plowed into tree trunks and rocks until I finally smacked into a chain-link fence that marked the end the park and the beginning of houses. The boundary between the two made any animal with sense think twice about taking another step.

At least once a day mothers warned their youngsters about stepping across that boundary. Outside the park were dogs and cats that could be the end of you, and I'm not talking about any kind of happy end, either.

Outside the park were lawnmowers and weed whackers that could also be the end of you, or at least scar you for life. And that's not even mentioning cars and trucks and any number of other human things that Gus claimed could leave you wheezing or fried or leaking all over the place, things like insecticides and electrical wires and even guns.

All that's why I pulled up at the fence to listen and sniff and stay absolutely still as a mouse who's lost his lucky seed.

For the first time that day I was glad it was blizzarding. The falling snow hid me from all the dangers on the other side of the fence.

The blurry outline of a swing set rose before me, marking a house whose kids had slingshots. My usual hole beneath the fence was nearby, though finding it in the snow took some work. What's more, the storm had knocked out all the street and house lights that usually blazed atop that hill. Lights were working elsewhere in the city, spreading their twilighty murk across the sky, but right where I stood, nothing was lit up. The storm made it impossible to make out the back of the house before me. That was both good and bad. They couldn't see me, but I couldn't see them either.

Finally, I bumped into the corner post, which told me exactly where I was. Soon I was wiggling under the wire fence and making my way to Ruth's, feeling more mole than possum. The hot tub that was my usual landmark in her backyard was nothing but a mound of snow, but I found it and angled toward the maple whose middle bough would lead me to Ruth's bedroom window.

I clawed my way up the wet tree trunk and plopped myself onto a branch, where I held up to catch my breath. Ghostly white as everything was, I couldn't even make out the ground beneath me. Ruth's house was mostly lost too. Usually, a computer or TV screen cast a homey glow out her second-floor window. But in the blackout, all that lit her room was a faint light at the end of the snow-covered limb stretching out before me.

I shuffled along until the bough began to sway beneath me. Afraid it might snap from all the added weight, I inched forward after that, creeping closer until able to see through the frosted glass. Ruth and her older brother were snacking on crackers while playing a game of cards by the glow of a flashlight. I happened to know they were playing cards because there was an old man in a house not too far away who day and night watched people do it on TV. Gus had pointed him out to me.

Wrapping my tail around the branch, I stretched out to scratch on the window. A voice stopped me cold before I reached the glass. It came from behind me.

"Just where do you think you're going?"

It startled me so bad that I lost my grip and nearly fell. To save myself I ended up clinging upside down from the tree. There wasn't any need to check over my shoulder or between my legs to find out who'd snuck up on me. There were only a couple of someones in the park who ever bothered following me anywhere, and I knew for a fact that I could rule out Mayor Crawdaddy. He was the one who'd sent me on this fool's errand. That left the Earl of Sussex. Making the mayor take an oath not to tell him where I was going had been a strategical error. It only made Sussex all the more curious.

"You're interfering with official business," I said with as much dignity as I could muster while hanging upside down.

"Since when has spying on humans been official business?"

"Who's spying? I'm here to find out if that kid in there might know anything about the big galumpus chewing on twigs back in the bog."

"Now, why would some human know about that?" Sussex never gave humans any credit, having the same low opinion of them as he did of chipmunks.

Rather than argue about it, I jerked a paw toward the window and asked, "Can't you read what it says on that kid's cap?"

I figured I was on safe ground. No way was Sussex going to admit that he couldn't read what it said on the billed cap Ruth was wearing. Mayor Crawdaddy liked to claim he could read human signs around the park, so Sussex bragged about it too. But whenever you got right down to it, neither of them could read a single sign, except maybe those big red ones that might say STOP. Often as not, people in cars seemed to stop at them.

But sometimes drivers blew right past those signs, so who knew for sure what the word on it meant? Not the mayor, or Sussex, or me.

"Which cap?" Sussex asked, squinting toward the window.

All right, he had me there. Ruth's brother was wearing one, too, except that his had fancy wool earflaps and no writing on its front.

"The one that says *galumpus* on it," I answered, pretending I could read right along with everyone else. "The kid wearing it is supposed to be some kind of world-famous expert on galumpuses. So me and the mayor thought she might be able to help us figure out what to do with that one in the bog."

Sussex left that alone. What else could he do? Without admitting that he couldn't read, I mean.

"Do you have any idea how dangerous approaching her could be?" Sussex challenged.

"Some," I allowed, sort of skipping over how many times I'd paid Ruth a visit on this very branch. "But for the good of the park and everyone in it, I'm willing to risk it."

"Why do I get the idea that you and Crawdaddy know more than you're letting on?"

"What are you talking about?" I grunted, struggling to flip myself right-side up.

"Somehow you knew right where to find a galumpus expert," Sussex pointed out. "How?"

I hated to admit it, but Earl deserved some credit. He'd zoomed right in on the weakest point of my story. It looked as though I'd have to get my paws on him and try to talk some sense into him, or he'd be telling the whole park I was consorting with humans. Failing that, I'd have to somehow bribe him to keep his mouth shut. But I never got a chance to do either. We'd been talking too loud. The window I'd been working toward got thrown open and a voice called out a greeting.

"Uncle Fester!"

Behind me, Sussex disappeared faster than a wisp of smoke.

Chapter 7

She's Got a Blanket!

"Uncle Fester!" Ruth cried again, happy as ever to see me.

Of course, she shared a whole bunch more, too, though I had no idea what she was saying. Her tone said she was probably scolding me for being out in a blizzard. On top of sounding glad to see me, she also sounded shocked to find me snow-caked and shivering outside her window.

She was a skinny kid with lots of elbows and knees

and long dark hair that she kept tucked behind her ears, which were real handy for that 'cause of the way they stuck out. When she got excited, her cheeks flushed and her eyes jigged around and her voice squeaked up.

"We could use a little help down in the bog," I said, still hanging upside down from the branch.

Why I bothered to say that, I'm not sure. She wouldn't have understood a word of it. I only knew that her name was Ruth because her older brother yelled it at her so often, and I knew that she thought my name was Uncle Fester because she said it every time she saw me. And that summed up how many words we shared. I was awful worked up, though, and I jabbered away as if she knew exactly what I was going on about. I kept it up until her brother shouted at us. As usual, the only thing I could pick out of what he had to say was her name.

"Ruth!"

He seemed upset about something, probably me. The few times we'd crossed paths he treated me like a ferocious beast who could tear down houses and uproot trees. He was a shouty guy, not the sort who'd ever think of inviting a poor, shivering woodland creature indoors to warm up. Taller than Ruth and having sprouted a scraggy mustache, he loved to carry on as if in charge.

Leaning out her window, Ruth whispered something kindly to me, but her brother clomped across the room to push her aside and close the window. He was blustering so loudly, you might have thought he was saving her life.

Ruth threw some angry words back at him.

As soon as Ruth wasn't looking, I opened my mouth as wide as I could, which is awfully wide, and hissed at her brother. Possums have a fearsome number of sharp teeth. I showed him my hackles, too.

It worked.

The brother fled the room, taking the flashlight with him.

But it worked too well. Ruth followed him. I could hear them bickering all the way down a stairs. That left me hanging from a branch, totally alone, except for my thoughts. No need to go into those—they were a snivelly, pitiful bunch.

Ruth and her brother were gone so long that I nearly called it quits, but finally Ruth returned with what Gus calls a dinner roll. After reopening the window, she set it on the ledge. Normally I would have grabbed that roll no questions asked, but I'd come calling in my official capacity as Mayor Crawdaddy's assistant and didn't have time to be snarfing up delicacies. No, I leveraged myself back onto the branch, teetered a bit, got my balance, and waved for Ruth to follow me. That motion had worked when I'd been sent to get help for the little girl who'd been lost in the woods, though then I'd been dealing with a dog. He probably would have followed me without any wave at all.

"Uncle Fester," she coaxed, holding the roll out the window.

It pained me to ignore that treat, but I backed farther away and again waved for her to follow me.

She tried some baby talk. Humans are awfully big on it, as if it will help us understand them. To show her that I meant business, I inched farther away and went through the follow-me routine yet again.

"Uncle Fester," she scolded.

When I kept my distance, she left the window to disappear into her closet, where she dug out a hockey stick.

Wicked things, those. In the wrong hands, I mean. But Ruth just balanced the dinner roll on the curved end of it and stuck it out the window to reach me.

That's when I found out she'd smeared crunchy peanut butter on that roll! When it came to any kind of peanut butter, I was weak, and the crunchy stuff nearly wiped out my last bit of willpower. All that kept me from thinking of what would happen if I failed. The mayor would never let me hear the end of it, that's what. And Sussex was sure to be watching all this from a nearby tree, eager to file a report with anyone who had ears. To save myself from that, I swatted the stick away, maybe a little harder than I should have. The dinner roll went flying. Me too, much as a possum can fly. Off the branch I tumbled, heavy as a rock. Even my tail couldn't save me. I whipped it around the branch but couldn't hold on.

"Uncle Fester!" Ruth gasped, grabbing for me and missing.

Good thing all that pillowy snow waited down below. I sank into it as if landing on an old couch deep in the woods. Soon as I hit, my body spazzed out on me. My eyes rolled up and filled with stars. I went rigid and smelled woodsmoke and heard the tinkling of glass wind chimes . . . all sure signs that I was about to play dead. Couldn't help myself. No possum could.

"Uncle Fester?" Ruth cried out, leaning out the window to see if I was okay.

Bless her heart. She came to my rescue as quick as she could, though first she had to tug on all the stuff that people wear instead of fur—boots and coats and mittens and stocking caps—as well as slip on the backpack she always carried treats inside. By the time she'd clattered downstairs and barged out the back door, I'd roused myself and shaken off the fall to struggle out of the snowdrift.

"Uncle Fester?" Ruth asked, getting a little closer than I liked.

I bared my teeth and hissed till she backed off. Sorry, instinct. Turning away from Ruth, I staggered toward the park with as busted-up a limp as I could muster. I went for broke on the whimpering, too.

"Uncle Fester!" she cried.

She came after me, coaxing me back, but I kept

lurching out of her reach. I'd lured her about halfway to the park fence before she gave up with a frustrated cry and rushed back into her house. Afraid that I'd lost her, I squealed up a storm until she burst back outside with a dark blue blanket. I knew because Sussex sounded the alarm from a nearby tree.

"She's got a blanket! She's got a blanket!"

All of a sudden my legs started working fine and I scrambled for the fence, throwing off whimpers as I went.

Ruth cried out in frustration and tossed the blanket like a net, hoping to catch me beneath it, but I didn't let her get close enough for that to work. The falling snow and drifts helped with that, hiding me and slowing her. Diving through my hole under the fence, I surfaced on the other side, wailing as if about to die.

At the same time, Ruth's brother stuck his head out the back door to yell something at her. When that didn't slow her down, he ducked inside to grab the trumpet that he was awfully proud of. Once or twice before I'd heard him blow on that horn to call Ruth home from the park. As a rule, she didn't pay it much mind, and this time

wasn't any dif-
ferent—she kept
right on coming to
the rescue. Naturally,
Sussex was all over that.

"She's still coming! She's still
coming!"

Pulling herself to the top of the fence, Ruth flopped
over into the park. Good thing I'd cleared out or she'd
have squashed me flatter than . . . Well, I don't like to
think what I might have been flatter than, except to say
that stuff that flat sometimes decorates the road after
some poor animal trusted one of those signs that sup-
posedly said *stop*.

From there she tracked me down the hill, casting her blanket at me from time to time as she called out to me.

"Uncle Fester!"

Sussex made a contribution. "Mad girl!" he heralded from the treetops. "Mad girl!"

And Ruth's brother got in on the act, too, with his trumpet, calling for his younger sister to come back. No way did he practice as much as he should have on that thing. His wheezy notes faded away before we reached the bottom of the hill.

Chapter 8

The Smokey 3000

We got back to the bog just in time, though I wasn't exactly sure in time for what. The galumpus and everyone else was standing exactly where I'd left them, looking as though they'd been trapped in a snow globe while I was gone. That slowed me down considerably. Something wasn't right.

Even more wrongish was how quiet everyone had fallen, even the Earl of Sussex. He'd quit sounding the alarm about Ruth to get an eyeful of what was waiting for us. His eyes weren't the only ones getting filled, either. No one even noticed Ruth skidding to a stop behind me, and a human charging out of the woods normally had everyone diving for the handiest scrap of cover.

Heavy as the snow was coming down, it took me a bit to figure out what was going on. When I did, it grabbed me by the gizzard, same as it had everyone else.

Someone new had joined the party.

She was standing beside Twigs, patting the big galumpus's shoulder hump and comforting him in a soft, everything-will-be-all-right kind of way. Poor Twigs was honking that long nose of his and looking powerfully saggy around the knees, as if about to crumple.

The newcomer stood on her hind legs and was dressed like a human in a park ranger's brown uniform that had a brass name tag on the breast pocket. Up top, she wore a round hat. Pinned to her hatband was a luminous yellow flower, a black-eyed Susie that was way, way out of season and was rotating back and forth like some kind of backyard camera. Not a single snowflake stuck to the flower's bright petals. For that matter, there wasn't any snow sticking to the rest of her, either. Her eyes had a violet shimmer to them, and there's probably one other thing I should mention about her—she was covered with green fur that glowed like willow leaves on a sunny spring day.

By then Ruth had caught up to me.

"Uncle Fester!" she panted.

The rest of what Ruth had to say trailed off as she took in all the animals gathered beneath the tamaracks—the wild turkeys, the woodchucks, the cardinals. When her eyes reached what the rest of us were ogling, she fell silent as a maple leaf. After a moment, she did think of something to say, though her tone sounded awfully unsure. Fortunately, a new voice spoke up, filling in the blanks.

"Class," the green-furred park ranger called out to us. She also clapped her paws to get our attention, though that was hardly necessary. "The young girl who's just joined us wants to know if I'm a green bear."

We gasped and shrank back. Were the old stories true? The ones the gray tails loved to scare kits and chicks with? Did the restless ghost of a bear from olden days wander through the woods of Theodore Wirth on

72

stormy nights? And a green bear at that. A green bear who addressed us as her class? We didn't have time to decide if we were spooked or giddy. The creature bowed politely and answered Ruth in a honey-filled human voice that made you long to hear her go on longer, even if you were trembling in a blizzard and didn't understand a word of what she was spewing. A moment later she translated what she'd told Ruth.

"Class," she said, "I told her that I am indeed a green bear. A Smokey 3000 Park Ranger model, at your service."

Ruth said something real slow then, as if she didn't want there to be any mistakes made.

"She wants to know if I'm talking to you," the Smokey 3000 Park Ranger model chuckled kindly. "I shall tell her that I am."

And the green bear made some more human words.

"Hold on now," Sussex butted in. "Why can't we see through you?"

The green bear blinked her violet eyes for several seconds, as if searching deep inside herself for the correct answer. Naturally, we were all blinking, too, especially

Ruth. She didn't look at all used to red squirrels chattering at green bears.

"I'm afraid I don't understand," the Smokey 3000 finally said to the Earl of Sussex. "Could you please rephrase your question?"

"You bet I can," Sussex said. "Shouldn't we be able to see through a ghost?"

"But I'm not a ghost, sir."

Ruth interrupted, sounding more excited than I'd ever heard her before. The green bear answered her before translating for us: "She wants to know if the red squirrel asked me a question."

"What'd you tell her?" Mayor Crawdaddy asked, turning suspicious. Any time the mayor felt left out of the loop, watch out.

"I told her yes," the green bear answered. "That I am programmed to understand seven thousand, four hundred, and twenty-two languages, including North American Animal Speech. I also told her that he asked if I was a ghost."

"Are you sure you're not a ghost?" Gigi asked, wanting to be sure.

"Absolutely, ma'am."

That eased Gigi's mind, but it also started a flutter and chirp as everyone took a crack at guessing just what the green bear might be if she wasn't a ghost. All the babbling had Ruth twisting every which way until Mayor Crawdaddy finally raised his voice to call for order.

"If you're not a ghost," the mayor asked, "just what in high fiddly are you?"

"A robot," answered the Smokey 3000.

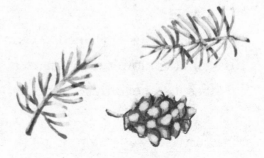

Chapter 9

Ten Thousand Years

If hearing that she wasn't a ghost triggered an uproar, learning that she was a robot doubled it.

"A what?"

"Robot," Gus explained. "A kind of machine like a truck or lawnmower, only smarter."

"Has it come to this?"

"Isn't anywhere safe?"

Everyone was tugging on a neighbor's wing or

poking their flank, and talking louder to be heard, and getting more excited by the second.

"What'd Gus say?"

"Who's Roy Bot?"

"Does anyone know what's going on?"

The ballyhoo lasted until Ruth tugged off her mittens, hooked her fingers in the corners of her mouth, and whistled for quiet. Boy, did she get it. Every head jerked her way at once. She took advantage of the opening to trade words with the green bear, who eventually switched to animal talk to bring us up to date on what they'd been saying.

"She wants to know what kind of robot I am."

"There's more than one kind?" the mayor beefed. The mournful look on his masked face was growing deeper.

"Yes, indeed, class," the 3000 answered. "There are a multitude of robots in my time. I informed this girl that I am an educational model, what some call a teacher or synapse minder. I've been modified to conduct field trips for students of all ages. The young woman also wanted to know if Twigs was a robot."

"I'm not, am I?" Twigs asked, shocked.

"Certainly not. I told her you were a woolly mammoth."

Fast as everyone's head whipped toward Twigs, the big galumpus checked over his shoulder as if we were all gawking at someone behind him. Realizing his mistake, he turned frontward and sheepishly said, "That's what I thought."

"W-what's a woolly mammoth?" squeaked the chipmunk named Opie.

"Class," the 3000 patiently explained, "the closest relative of a woolly mammoth in your time period would be an elephant."

"It would?" Opie asked, which was a polite way of saying he had no idea what the green bear was talking about. "Do they have those same kind of long noses?"

"The correct term for this woolly mammoth's nose is *proboscis* or *trunk*. And the answer is yes."

"That sounds right," Gus agreed.

None of us but Gus knew anything more about elephants than we did about woolly mammoths, and he didn't know much more. "They get big," he said.

And what had the green bear meant by *time period*?

While we were trying to come to grips with all that, Ruth and the green bear talked back and forth. At the end of which, the 3000 told us that Ruth had asked if woolly mammoths weren't extinct.

Gus didn't speak up to tell us what *extinct* meant, and I was sure that nobody else in the park had ever heard of it either. And now that we had heard of it, we didn't like the sound of it. Something about it seemed sharp and gritty in our mouths as we repeated it. And yet we all sat around nodding as if we'd had the same thought about woolly mammoths ourselves, especially Sussex.

Even though I'd seen a nature show or two on TV, my head-nodding soon slowed. I hated being a stickler, but if there was one thing that being Mayor Crawdaddy's assistant had taught me, it was that words matter. Many's the time he'd leaped on some poorly chosen word I'd used and turned it to his advantage. So in the name of accuracy, I raised a question that everyone else was ducking.

"What exactly does *extinct* mean?"

"That an animal no longer lives anywhere on earth."

"Why, that sounds terrible," Gigi said, shocked.

"Where do they live?" my cousin Frasier asked.

"They don't," the 3000 answered. "They've ceased to live anywhere."

"Numbskull," Sussex spliced in as if he'd known that all along.

"Hold on now," Mayor Crawdaddy weighed in. "Before we all start dithering away, I'd like to point out that this galumpus here doesn't look too extinctified to me."

"That would be correct, sir," the Smokey 3000 respectfully agreed, "for the moment. He is standing here before you because of a temporal displacement incident."

Nobody bothered nodding as if they had the slightest idea of what that was. Well, almost nobody.

"Didn't we have one of those just last week?" Sussex horned in, unable to be left out of anything, even a temporal displacement incident, without pretending he was some kind of expert.

"Let's not get all carried away," the mayor said, trying to calm Earl down. "But it might be a good idea, Ms.

Smokey 3000, if you took a moment to tell us exactly where you and the galumpus are from."

We were all agreed on that.

"Class," the green bear informed us, "I'm from the future. This woolly mammoth is from the past."

Now, that struck me as a slippery kind of answer to what should have been a simple question. Mayor Crawdaddy shot me a jealous look that said he wished he'd come up with a whopper that size himself. The only one nodding as if it made perfect sense was Sussex.

"How far in the future?" I asked, just to make it seem as if my mouth was hanging open for a reason.

"Approximately ten thousand, seven hundred, and ninety-eight years, six months, twenty-three days, nineteen hours, six minutes, and forty-two seconds, although that could be off by a few millennia. The temporal displacement that cast us here created an enormous electrical storm that fried a few of my components."

"And how far in the past?"

"Oh, exactly the same amount of time." The 3000 spoke as if that was elementary.

"And just how in creation did the two of you happen to end up here?" the mayor wanted to know.

"I was giving a tour of the last glacial age. It would appear that something went wrong."

"What kind of tour?" I said, not exactly following.

Now and then we saw groups of schoolkids in Theodore Wirth, but I'd yet to see one of them led by a willow-green bear in a park ranger's outfit.

"A middle school science class," the 3000 explained. "They were doing a unit on the last ice age and were visiting our temporal interpretive center for a firsthand look."

"There you go again," the mayor snorted. "I'm beginning to think you're working up to selling us something."

"Oh no," the 3000 assured us. "I'm strictly an educational unit."

"Then why don't you educate us on what a temporal interpretive center is? And what it has to do with us."

Several animals thought that sounded like a fine idea, which puffed the mayor up beyond the usual. If the snow falling on us hadn't been so heavy, I do believe he might have floated away.

"Class," the 3000 said, raising her voice be heard, "the temporal interpretive center was created to help students understand historical events."

"Such as?" Crawdaddy pushed.

"We visit any number of time periods here in the park. In this case, I was showing a class the conditions at the end of the last glacial period, what scientists call the Pleistocene."

"And just what were those conditions?" The mayor made it sound as though he didn't believe any of it.

"The park was drier and colder, though not a lot colder. Also, there were far fewer people, as well as a different range of animals that included woolly mammoths like our friend here."

She patted Twigs on the head.

"And when was all this?" I asked, having a little trouble keeping up.

"As I said, approximately ten thousand years ago. My calculations indicate that your current time stands at the midway point between my time in the future and Twigs's time in the past."

"My stars," said Gigi, neatly summing up what all of us were feeling.

"And where exactly are all these students you're teaching about these far-gone times?" the mayor asked.

"Back in the interpretive center," the 3000 assured us. "Time travel can be kind of touchy for biologics such as yourselves—rashes, nasal congestion, occasional rapid aging—so robots such as myself are sent to broadcast back images, sounds, smells. It's safer."

"So, what? They're back in the classroom watching us on TV?"

That grabbed everyone's attention. My vainer neighbors were all of a sudden slicking back their hair and fluffing their feathers and brushing their eyebrows to look better for the cameras, which they were casting about for. My shier neighbors had stepped behind a tree or tucked their heads under a wing or arm.

"Well, no," the 3000 said. "They're not watching you at the moment. The electrical storm I mentioned—"

"Here we go again," the mayor muttered, making sure he said it just loud enough for everyone to hear.

"—the one that fried some of my components and threw us here? It also damaged the system that transmits data back to my time."

"Are you trying to say you're stranded here?" asked the mayor.

Chapter 10

Haywire

The 3000 processed the mayor's question a moment before saying, "Stranded? Yes, for now."

"So those students you mentioned, they can't see us at all?"

"Correct."

Everyone but Ruth slouched a bit. The only reason she didn't bother relaxing was that she didn't know what we'd been gabbing about until the 3000 translated for her. When the 3000 and Ruth were done talking, the mayor had a follow-up question for the green bear.

"But if they could see us, they'd be watching us on some sort of TV?"

"A rough approximation, but yes. A three-dimensional TV."

"There you go again," the mayor chided, as if the 3000 was making it all up.

"Makes sense to me," Sussex couldn't resist saying.

No one paid Sussex any mind, which delighted the chipmunks.

"The students are in a large auditorium surrounded by holographic projections of what I transmit back. To them it seems as if they're standing in a meadow, or in the midst of a herd of woolly mammoths, or whatever my sensors were picking up."

"I'll just bet," Mayor Crawdaddy scoffed.

Everybody crowded a bit closer together, though, just in case.

"If everything was working," my cousin Frasier asked with a shiver, "could they touch us?"

"No, not at all. If they tried to, their hand would go right through you."

"As if we're ghosts," a mouse named Voltron said with a shiver.

"So how'd that big galumpus standing next to you get involved in all this?" the mayor asked.

"One of the students on the tour requested a close-up of a woolly mammoth, so I was approaching this one when a storm moved in, disrupting my temporal slipstream with a mega-voltage lightning strike. I found myself transported to this time. Apparently I was close enough to this fellow to pull him along with me."

"I saw you step out of nowhere," Twigs volunteered, "looking all shimmery."

"That was due to supercharged ions in the atmosphere," the green bear explained.

"You were scary."

"Sorry. I didn't mean to be. Normally I wouldn't have revealed myself at all."

All very fascinating, I'm sure. And the 3000 wasn't done, either. She went on to tell us how the trip at the Theodore Wirth Wildlife and Time Preservation

Sanctuary, as she called it, had gone wrong. She and Twigs had gotten separated when several of her subroutines started looping after she'd crash-landed in our time.

"Is that why your fur keeps flickering?" asked the Earl of Sussex.

Well, of course I'd noticed the same thing myself but had been too polite to bring it up. But every once in a while the 3000's green fur shimmered slightly, briefly glowing brighter, then dimmer, but it happened so quickly, in a blink, really, that I wasn't sure it'd happened at all.

"That would be correct," the 3000 agreed. "I'm continuing to have problems with the subroutines that control my appearance. That's why you're seeing me in my most recent mode. Extensive testing has proven that middle school students react favorably to robots in this form."

"Green fur and all?" I asked.

"This shade of green relaxes students, thus making them more receptive to learning."

"Too bad we're not middle school students," the mayor pointed out.

"Yes, a pity. I do apologize for not changing into a shape that's conducive for this conversation."

"What kind of shape might that be?" Sussex asked.

"We've found flying squirrels to be an effective appearance for talking to woodland creatures such as yourselves."

Naturally that was well received by the flying squirrels present, though Mayor Crawdaddy begged to differ.

"I'd like to see you pull that one off," the mayor said. "A flying squirrel your size would be one for the record books."

"You misunderstand," the 3000 answered. "I wouldn't be my current size. I'd present as the same size as your average flying squirrel."

"And just how are you going to manage that?"

"Optical refraction."

"Would your fur still be green?" asked a flying squirrel named Rocky.

"Yes. Green's best."

"As far as excuses go," the mayor complimented, "you've got a keeper there. The next time I'm in need of one, I'm going to—"

A bloodcurdling howl from the far side of the quaking bog cut him short. The sound pricked everyone's ears considerable. It wasn't the kind of howl that any of us had ever heard in the park before. One look at Gus confirmed that. Worried glances were getting passed around faster than sparrows can flit.

Even Ruth jerked toward the direction of the howl, and she asked a question.

"She's wondering if that was a wolf," the 3000 said.

"It better not have been," Mayor Crawdaddy said.

Theodore Wirth didn't have any wolves living in it, at least not in our time. Stories about wolf packs were handed down same as the ones about bears, except they were scarier. The closest we came to wolves were stray dogs and small packs of coyotes that passed through now and then and the occasional fox with visions of grandeur.

"My auditory sensors confirm that the howl originated from a human who was imitating a wolf," said the 3000.

Just then another howl rose from a different direction. Followed by a third howl from yet another direction.

The yellow flower in the 3000's hatband was rotating back and forth, trying to pinpoint locations. Everyone's head was whipping one way or another too.

Ruth spoke again and the 3000 translated, saying, "She's wondering if it's her brother and his friends trying to be funny."

Personally, I wasn't ready to start laughing, especially after the 3000 added, "I told her that it's most likely the cavemen I saw stalking this young woolly mammoth back in the Pleistocene. They were getting awfully close just before the time continuum went haywire."

"What's *haywire*?" Twigs asked.

"Robot talk," the mayor told him when Gus didn't speak up.

"What are cavemen?" asked Gus, sounding fascinated.

"I can answer that," Twigs offered. "They're those people who shout at us and poke at us and run away when we try to talk to them."

"And just why are they called *cave* men?" the mayor pressed. "Fill us in on that, if you can."

"The name comes from their tendency to take shelter

in caves," the 3000 answered. "It's a general term for early people."

"Are they related to the people around here now?" I asked.

"Search me," Twigs said.

"It's certainly possible, though difficult to say with one hundred percent accuracy," the 3000 answered. "Humans have always moved around a good deal."

"If they're related, we can't trust them," declared Sussex.

"Sometimes that would be true," the 3000 agreed. "Sometimes not."

"Isn't that helpful?" Mayor Crawdaddy fumed. "Got any other tidbits to share about them?"

"Someday their offspring will travel to Mars."

"Now, why would they want to go and do something like that?"

"Class, I believe that is a topic for another time."

The 3000 had a point. Right about then we heard a whoop that snatched away any thoughts about what those cavemen's descendants might be up to.

Chapter 11

A Wolf, a Cat, a Boar

Then came another whoop! followed by a third, altogether closer *whoop!*

Out of the snowy whiteness sprang a wolf, or at least that's what I guessed he was. He looked sort of familiar from a nature show I'd watched at Ruth's. He had a head like a dog's, though bigger and bristlier. The teeth flashing our way were enough to make me start playing dead any second. I could feel the tingles coming on fast and smelled woodsmoke rolling over me. It didn't leave me thinking too highly of the Smokey 3000's auditory sensors. I wasn't exactly sure what a caveman should look like, or sound like, but I had my doubts he'd be anything like this.

Nobody needed to holler *Scatter!* It was everyone for his- or herself. Bodies went flying pell-mell. Ruth got tangled up with a family of cottontails and lost her blanket. I knocked over a chipmunk and got bowled over by the mayor, who got flattened by a buck.

Screeches . . . whistles . . . grunts—we had 'em all.

The wolf was snapping and spraying snow and jabbing a long sharp spear in at least seventeen different directions. I sure never would have guessed that a wolf with that many teeth and claws needed to bother with a spear. Come to think of it, I wouldn't have ever guessed that they owned a spear. That seemed like a human kind of thing.

I headed for the nearest tree to climb but never made it. Hearing a terrible squeal from Twigs, I skidded to a stop and looked back, just in time to see the woolly mammoth covering his eyes with that nose of his, as if that would hide him. It worked about as well as his pretending to be invisible had.

Somewhere in there I saw the 3000 lift her willow-green paw. A bright beam of matching green light shot out the palm of that paw. It made the falling snow sparkle as it blasted the wolf's chest and blew him backward through the air as easy as a leaf. He smacked into a tree trunk and was knocked out cold.

Something told me that the 3000 probably didn't have trouble with the class clowns.

"What was that?" cried Mayor Crawdaddy, impressed despite himself.

"A Newtonian force beam," explained the 3000.

I wish I could say that wolf stayed down long enough for all of us to get away, but we'd barely gathered our wits when another wolf howled from a new direction. Things were sliding from bad to worse in such a downhill hurry that I barely had time to remember that somewhere or other I'd heard that wolves traveled in packs.

Two seconds later the biggest cat I ever hope to see lurched our way as if spit out by the blizzard. Sliding to a stop, he stomped a foot down and screamed at the sky as if throwing a tantrum.

"That's the cat!" Twigs cried.

Nobody bothered asking which cat. It looked as though the galumpus had been telling the truth about being chased by a kitty. Excuse me for nitpicking, but I sure didn't remember hearing anything on the grapevine about oversized cats traveling with wolves.

The cat spun around to glower in the direction he'd just been flung from. He shouted something, too. Whatever he was going on about, he wasn't saying it in animal talk. Wild as it may seem, that cat talked like a human.

Good thing we couldn't see who he was shouting at. Whatever had thrown a kitty that size didn't promise to be puny, and the blizzard had already spit out one huge, human-talking cat, a wolf, a green bear in a park ranger's uniform, and a big galumpus. Who knew what other surprises it held?

"He's saying he won't do it," the 3000 announced, in case any of us were wondering.

It figured that a green robot bear who could

understand over seven thousand languages wouldn't have any trouble with a cat talking human. Naturally the mayor acted as if the 3000 was showing off.

"Won't do what?" he crossly asked.

The 3000 didn't get around to answering that. A crumpled pop can came flying out of the woods first. It bounced off the cat's head and fell to the ground. The cat scrambled away from it as if the thing had teeth, sharp ones. Keeping his distance, he squinted at the can for a few seconds, breathing fast. The suspicious way he was sniffing and eyeballing that can had me guessing that such things didn't clutter up the bog ten thousand years ago. After a bit he nudged the can with his toe.

A word about that toe: It was covered by a home-made boot that looked all warm and fuzzy and made out of rabbit fur. Since when had cats started wearing those?

When the pop can didn't snap back at him, he kicked it clear out of sight as if getting even. Being tricked that way goaded him into turning on Twigs and the 3000, as if it was their fault that he'd been shown up by a pop can. He started toward them with a mealy-mouthed snarl, shouting as if they were in his way and he was trying to scare them off. Or maybe he was the one who was afraid. I wasn't exactly sure how upset, oversized kitty-cats behaved.

He sounded terribly ferocious, especially when I noticed that he had two fangs as big and sharp as knives. Just like the wolf, he carried a spear, though he kept his pointed at the ground, acting reluctant to use it.

Wolves with spears? Cats with spears? I was starting to notice a trend.

If possible, the cat's spear was longer and pointier than the wolf's. That thing looked as though it could have run through a half dozen trees without slowing down.

I sure felt sheepish for thinking that being afraid of some little kitty made Twigs yellow-bellied. Fast as everybody else was diving for cover? They were probably feeling the same way.

The only one not clearing out was Ruth. She stood right in the cat's path, shouting at him. I'd seen humans pull stunts like that on TV. Standing your ground when you should have been running for your life seemed to be a large part of movies, though that's just a possum's view. But I'll mention something else that happened on TV too—shouting. People liked to shout as they held their ground, just the way Ruth was doing right then, as if she had something to prove.

"She's asking if he's supposed to be a saber-toothed tiger," the 3000 translated for us.

There weren't any chipmunks left around to ask what the heck that was. The Earl of Sussex was also long gone. Gus had left too. But whatever a saber-toothed tiger was, Ruth would have been easy pickings if the 3000 hadn't come to the rescue again.

Up went the park ranger's green paw. Out poured the green beam. The Newtonian whatchamacallit caught that saber-toothed tiger in midroar. The beam tossed the kitty backward, all the way into the bog's pond of dark water. It flung him so far and so hard that it knocked his head clear off. I checked twice just to be sure.

That wasn't anywhere near as awful a sight as I would have thought. Believe it or not, that cat had a spare head inside the one it'd lost. The second head belonged to a boy, a scraggly-bearded, tangle-haired boy who didn't look much older than a cub himself.

For a second I thought the tiger must have swallowed a young caveman in one gulp. Now, we both know that doesn't make any sense, not as loud as the boy's head was screaming. What made more sense was that we hadn't been attacked by a cat at all but by a boy wearing a cat skin for a hat and robe. Frantic as he was sputtering and gasping and thrashing around in the pond where he'd landed? Lucky for him it was shallow.

We weren't paying attention to the cat boy, though. The wolf who'd smacked into the tree was nearer to us and already coming around. A closer look at him said he was a man, too, one wearing a wolf head and skin.

"Imposters!" Sussex shouted from the safety of a tree.

Ruth kept her distance but did ask the cavemen a question. They shouted back as if they didn't understand her.

The 3000 told Ruth something and then repeated it to us. "Class, these are the cavemen I mentioned."

That green bear looked ready to launch into some educational explanation about time distortions and

102

slipstream blockage and misplaced years, but a third caveman put a stop to that by stepping out of the blizzard. He'd sneaked up directly behind the green bear in all the excitement. At a glance, he didn't look any more like a man than the first two. He had short tusks and had strung a bunch of crumpled pop cans and candy wrappers around his neck. I didn't find out until later that he was supposed to be a wild boar. Whatever he was, his necklace must have come from a trash can he'd rummaged through. He held a club, a big knobby, splattered, ugly thing that he gripped with both hands. Lifting it over his head, he smashed it down on top of the Smokey 3000's round hat without so much as a howdy.

The thunk that club made rang through the bog. The sound hit me like a blow and left me feeling powerfully sick, though that's nothing compared to what it did to the 3000. It put a sizeable dent in the robot's hat and made something inside her crackle in a kind of helpless way. I didn't see any sparks, but the black-eyed Susie in her hatband bent sideways as easy as a piece of wire. The bear's head spun around and lifted up as if about to pop off. Meanwhile, the blow also drove the green bear to her knees, from where she kind of tipped sideways without much of anything to say except "Reboot."

And guess what? That third caveman wasn't done making trouble. He heaved that club above his head again, as if about to lower the boom on Twigs.

What stopped him?

Ruth. She stepped forward, braver than all the rest of us put together. Out of a pocket she fumbled a phone, though not to talk into, the way people usually did. No, she held it in front of her like a camera, aiming it at the caveman wearing the tusked head. At the same time she yelled at him. She sounded as protective of Twigs as she did of me when her older brother was up to no good.

The shout made the cavemen glance her way just as Ruth clicked something on the phone. A blinding white light flashed in the caveman's face, scaring him worse than he'd scared us.

You could tell he'd never, ever seen anything explode that brightly before. He staggered backward, dropping the club to paw at his eyes as if they were on fire. The club fell behind him. He tripped over it and went down, the back of his head landing with a clunk on something buried in the snow, probably a tree root. He must have hit it hard, 'cause he didn't bounce back up.

"That'll teach 'em," Sussex declared from the safety of his tree, managing to sound as if he was the one who'd saved the day.

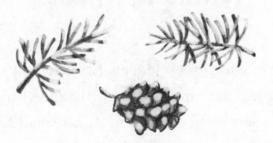

Chapter 12

Riding the Hump

Danger always gave Mayor Crawdaddy the get-up-and-goes, and sure enough, by the time I turned to ask him what we should do next, his small footsteps were already filling in with falling snow.

He wasn't the only one missing, either. The blizzard went right on wiping out the woods and the bog and the city that spread out around us. White upon white upon white. A barrage of lightning, followed by rumbling thunder, drowned out anybody who tried to speak up, though really, at the moment everyone was speechless as pinecones.

The cavemen hadn't completely disappeared, though. They were either flattened out on the ground, or slumped against a tree, or splashing about the bog's dark pond.

Ruth hadn't gone anywhere either. She kept spinning about as if unable to believe what had happened. Her mouth was forming words that I couldn't hear above the thunder. Her baffled expression said *This can't be!* Or maybe *Am I dreaming?* Or possibly *Enough, already!*

As the thunder dwindled, Twigs lifted his trunk off his eyes and *ha-room*ed through it, filling the bog with the most mournful, the most forlorn, the most awful and lost bugling ever heard in Theodore Wirth. The messing around that Ruth's brother did on that trumpet of his couldn't even begin to compete. It sounded to me as though Twigs was calling out to his home. A basket of abandoned puppies wouldn't have whimpered as pitiful.

As for the Smokey 3000, she was whirring and clanking and flickering like a rammed street sweeper.

As the thunder faded, I heard her say over and over, "Reboot. Reboot. Reboot. Reboot."

The way the snow kept coming down? Sussex was racing around as if the sky was falling. With the mayor missing in action, somebody had to step up, and pretty fast, too, or those three cavemen would find their legs and we'd be right back where we'd started. So I pumped myself up and pretended I was feeling brave.

"Pull yourselves together!" I shouted.

To my surprise, everybody stilled. Being yelled at by a possum was something new, and it caught them totally off-guard. Even Ruth, who wouldn't have had the slightest notion of what I was yelling about, quit spinning around to look at me.

"Who made you mayor?" the Earl of Sussex demanded.

"Crawdaddy did," I lied. "Right before he went for help."

"I didn't hear any such thing."

Me either, but I wasn't about to give Sussex an opening that big. The last time the mayor had gone for help . . . Well, there hadn't been any last time. It'd never happened. When it came to getting help, he was awfully prone to sending me.

"He did it while you were wailing nonstop about what a fix we were in," I told him.

"Who's he going to get?" Sussex jeered.

"He didn't have time to say. Now everybody listen up, please. We've got to get young Twigs out of here before these cavemen pull themselves together."

"Why do we need to worry about that?" Sussex balked. "Maybe they're here to take the galumpus home."

"I suppose that's why they brought their spears and clubs along," I said.

"Could be," Sussex reasoned. "Or maybe they just never go anywhere without them."

I was about to ask how he thought they got the skins they were wearing, but the 3000 had regained her senses and spoke up first.

"Class, please!" The 3000 clanked a bit before going on. "The possum's right. We need to move if we're to have any hope of getting this young woolly mammoth home."

"And just how are we supposed to do that?" Sussex squawked.

"By returning to the temporal vortex that dropped us here," said the 3000.

That had everyone scratching their heads but good.

"Would you mind breaking that down into littler words?" Sussex groused. "So we can figure out what you're going on about."

"The hole in time that we dropped out of," the 3000 explained.

"Forget it," Twigs stubbornly said. "I'm not going."

"I suppose you'd rather stay here and get to know those spears better?" said Sussex.

"Not going," the big galumpus repeated, digging in.

"What's this hole in time look like?" I asked the 3000.

"It's a massive, revolving portal that's framed by brilliant energy but filled with a black void. Lightning bolts arc inside it. The roar of time rushing out from it can at times be deafening."

Everybody's eyes were getting bulgier by the second.

"Any smell?" asked a rabbit who may have been

named Thumper. There were a lot of rabbits named Thumper in the park.

"A faint seepage from whatever time period it's connected to."

"Sounds like quite a party," Sussex snickered. "Anybody seen anything like that around here?"

Nobody raised a paw.

"Maybe you could just tell us where to go," I suggested.

"I wish I knew," the 3000 said, tapping above an ear to stop a rattle. "But that caveman's blow to my head appears to have smashed my memory banks and geo-positioning unit. I'm afraid that any data that could pinpoint where we entered your time period has been wiped out."

"Awful convenient," commented Sussex.

"But perhaps," the 3000 continued, "we could follow this woolly mammoth's footprints back to where he first arrived in the park? That ought to get us there."

"That'd be brilliant," Sussex scoffed, "except for one little thing."

"And what would that be?" I asked.

"This blizzard we're standing in. In case you hadn't noticed, it fills in footprints almost as fast as you can leave them, even if they're the size of this galumpus's."

"That does present a problem," the 3000 agreed.

"Too bad it's not our only problem," I said, pointing at the caveman wearing the wolf skin. He'd stood up and was rubbing the back of his head as if he didn't know where he was or what had hit him.

In a wink, animals were once again tearing off in the handiest direction they could find. There were collisions. Plenty of name-calling, too. This time I got knocked over by deer hooves and trampled by bunnies. When I got back to my feet, the only ones left in the bog were Twigs, the Smokey 3000, Ruth, and me.

"Come on, Twigs," I coaxed. "We've got to get you out of here."

The poor woolly was bawling so hard that I don't even know if he caught what I'd said. Scuttling over to him, I spoke into the end of his trunk, as if that might help him hear me.

"If you want to get home," I said into that trunk, "we've got to get moving."

"Home's gone," he blubbered.

But Ruth figured out what I was up to, even if she couldn't understand what I was saying, and slapped Twigs on his sizeable rump. That brought him to his senses, and he lurched forward in surprise. He would have trampled me for sure if I hadn't still been holding on to his trunk, which turned out to be surprisingly strong. In nothing flat he flung me over his head, where I landed on his humped shoulders and hung on to his shaggy hide for dear life.

"Whoa!" shouted someone behind us. "What about me?"

Glancing over my shoulder, I saw Mayor Crawdaddy stranded in the snow behind us. He'd been hiding beneath Twigs the whole while. He wasn't feeling the least bit sheepish about his disappearing act, not as loud as he bellowed for help. Same as ever, bold and brassy. All I can say is, I was powerfully glad to have him back. Being in charge was about as much fun as explaining water to a bluegill named Bart.

The mayor needn't have worried about being left behind, though. Twigs barely made it a half-dozen steps before braking to a stop. The wolf-skinned caveman had struggled to his feet and teetered crookedly before us, leaning on his spear.

"I thought you were getting help?" Sussex had returned to chide the mayor.

"Couldn't find any," answered Crawdaddy.

They might have had a good long blow about what kind of help the mayor expected to find under a woolly mammoth, but the 3000 spoke up first.

"Class," the green bear announced, "I'm afraid I find myself in need of additional assistance too. My optical sensors appear to be offline."

"What's that mean?" Sussex chattered from his perch.

"I can't see."

I must say, that robot took losing her sight right in stride. In a calm voice, she informed Ruth of her blindness. Ruth panicked briefly but got herself under control with some deep breaths, then took charge. I couldn't have been any prouder if I really was her uncle Fester.

After scooping up the mayor, Ruth tossed him onto Twigs's back right beside me. Then she led the 3000 forward by the arm until she could put Twigs's tail in the green bear's paw. The park ranger must have squeezed the woolly's tail a mite too hard. Twigs lurched forward, plowing right over the wolf caveman, who had to dive to the side or risk getting run through by a tusk.

Out of the bog we lumbered, me and the mayor holding on to Twigs's shaggy back for all we were worth. The 3000 loped along behind, gripping the woolly's tail and running on her hind legs in a seesaw kind of way. Ruth brought up the rear, stopping every now and then to check on what the cavemen were up to behind us and to scream something at us. We all took Ruth's shouts to mean, *Move it! Move it! Move it!*

As for Sussex—gone again.

It was rare when Mayor Crawdaddy couldn't think of some way to improve on somebody else's order, but we'd landed on such a day, though he did share one little thought.

"Gilly," he said through gritted teeth, "you've really

outdone yourself this time."

Not a single word of thanks did I get for trying to cover up his cowering under Twigs. That would have been too much to expect. But hearing his quip did reassure me of one thing: Ruth had tossed the right raccoon up beside me. Rather than waste energy defending myself, I asked, all innocent-like, "What? Aren't you glad you came?"

He growled at me. If visibility had been better that night, you might have seen me grinning for a split second.

The last thing I saw before leaving the bog? The caveman with the saber-toothed tiger skin—the one who was afraid of pop cans—had figured out that he didn't have to swim to save himself from drowning in the bog's small pond. All he had to do was stand up and wade to shore. While he did it, he was bellowing something wretched and woeful and tearful at the other two cavemen, something like *That's it! I'm done! This is too hard!*

One of the other cavemen barked something fiery back at the boy, something that must have been along the lines of *Oh no you're not!* Or *We'll see about that!* Or *Pull yourself together!*

After that, their shouts tangled together into one long, angry burst as we pulled away from them.

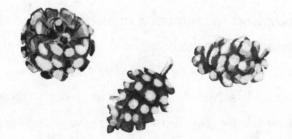

Chapter 13

Time Tunnels

We followed a mountain bike trail up the hill that stood between the bog and a road that cuts through our park. Not that we could see the trail. Two- or three-foot snowdrifts hid it, but the gap it cut between the trees showed the way. Though our every step carried us farther away from Ruth's house, she never complained a bit. Her only reaction was to sneak a peek over her shoulder now and then, as if she might be a tiny bit worried about what she'd been swept up in.

Twigs might not have been built for speed, but if there was one place where he was faster than anyone else, it had to be deep snow. He plowed through the stuff as if he was born for it.

"Ain't going home," the big galumpus muttered as we went. "Ain't going home. Ain't going . . ."

"You're doing fine," I encouraged. "Just keep it up. Everything will be all right."

"I've got a question," Mayor Crawdaddy announced once the cavemen's cries had died away. "Does anyone know where we're going?"

Occasionally the mayor surprised me with something sensible. It was rare but known to happen. We were perched side by side on Twigs's shaggy shoulders when he came up with that one. As full of nettles and gas as he sounded? I didn't need a bonfire to help me see that any second now he'd probably call it quits and hand this whole mess off to one of his assistants, namely me.

"To a time tunnel that will get this galumpus home," I reminded him.

"And which way might that be?" Crawdaddy asked.

"Or are we just going to wander around in circles, hoping to bump into it?"

His last question hung in the air without anyone trying to answer it. For a few seconds it seemed to snow even faster, if such a thing was possible. Visibility was already close to zero. At times I could barely see the ends of my whiskers. The tips of Twigs's tusks came and went from view. Though I hated to admit it, the mayor might have been right. At this rate, the only way we'd find something was by bumping into it. And we may have escaped the cavemen, but what good did that do if we had no idea where we were going?

"Ain't going home," Twigs stubbornly insisted.

And speaking of our escape, it was a flimsy one. Close as those cavemen were, they weren't going to have trouble following us. Woolly mammoths don't exactly tiptoe through snowdrifts, and even a blizzard would need several minutes to fill in our trail.

Luckily, the 3000 was built to take such problems all in stride. Calm as could be, she made a suggestion. "Twigs," the 3000 said, "can you remember what you saw when you first landed here?"

"Nope," Twigs said, furrowing his brow as if refusing to try.

"Come on now," I encouraged, seeing what the 3000 was getting at. "There must be a little something that comes to mind?"

The big galumpus shook his head stubbornly.

"Out with it," the mayor butted in.

The bullying made the big galumpus go all pigheaded. Batting at the falling snow with his trunk, he cried out indignantly, "Too much white stuff! I can't think!"

"Oh, folderol," the mayor said, dismissing Twigs's protests. "A little falling snow's the least of your worries. Now out with it. Which way should we be going? And try to remember that we're not exactly alone out here."

He was talking about the cavemen, who'd gone quiet behind us. Maybe they were too far away to be heard. Then again, maybe they were a whole lot closer than we knew, hidden by the falling snow.

"I remember my little sister," Twigs said unexpectedly, as if someone had accused him of forgetting her.

"She was tagging along same as always. The smoke scared her."

"What smoke?" the mayor said, alarmed. Living in a dead oak, he was always afraid of fire.

It seemed a simple enough question, but it made Twigs hang his head and blubber.

"There was a fire," the 3000 explained.

The way Twigs sagged when the 3000 said that? He sounded pinned beneath an avalanche with no hope of ever getting out.

"I started running," Twigs said at last. "There was all that smoke, and a storm was coming too. Lightning crashed right on top of us. Something picked me up and threw me."

"You ran into the time anomaly," the 3000 explained. "The storm's massive electrical discharge created it near where I'd entered your time."

"I tried to grab my little sister," Twigs went on, defensively, "but couldn't hold on to her. Whatever grabbed me wouldn't let go. My ma yelled at me from far away. I answered but I don't know if she heard me."

"I'll bet she did," I told him.

"Things got dark and prickly." Twigs shivered, remembering. "And cold."

"Time tunnels feel that way," said the 3000.

"I saw a bright light," Twigs went on. "It was sucking me toward it, and all of a sudden my feet touched ground again."

"Tell us about that," the 3000 said, as if it might be something useful. "If we can get back there soon enough, we should be able to follow it to the Pleistocene."

"Soon enough?" the mayor squawked. "Soon enough for what?"

"To get through the rip in time before it closes. Time tunnels tend to be unstable."

"Don't be telling us that," the mayor ordered.

"Class," the 3000 answered, "telling you something else would be inaccurate."

"How long do you figure we've got before this time tunnel closes?" I asked.

"A few hours at most."

"And what happens if we're late?' I asked.

"We'll be in need of a backup plan," said the 3000.

"You got one?"

"Presently, no."

The mayor weighed in: "So call up that interpretive center you're so proud of. You must have some gizmo for that. Tell them to come get you."

"Class," the 3000 patiently explained, "I believe I've already told you that the electrical storm damaged the system that allows me to communicate with my time. I'm afraid I'm temporarily out of touch with my support team."

"How temporarily?"

"Unknown."

"That seals it," fumed the mayor. Digging his claws into Twigs's back, he ordered, "You! Start remembering where you first landed."

"There was a cave," the big galumpus blurted, scared by the mayor's outburst. "I got chased out of it by those cavemen, who were right behind me. That's when I got lost until I got found. By you."

"That cave must be the entry point," the 3000 said.

"Well, that's just dandy," the mayor said. "Except for one little problem. There aren't any caves in this park."

Chapter 14

Mayday! Mayday!

"**Are you positive they're no caves** in the vicinity?" asked the 3000.

"Seems like something I'd remember," the mayor huffed.

"We could try asking Ruth," I suggested.

"By all means," the mayor said, offended, "ask the human."

So the Smokey 3000 quizzed Ruth about caves in

the park. She quickly learned that my friend didn't know of any and passed the news on to us.

"Like I said," muttered Mayor Crawdaddy.

That left us standing around straining to remember any kind of cave we'd heard of nearby. The wet, heavy snow didn't help us think any faster. We were also wondering just how near those cavemen had gotten.

"This is hopeless," moaned the mayor.

Ruth didn't sound ready for that much despair and asked a question.

"She wants to know what kind of cave it was," said the 3000.

"This conversation is getting intelligenter by the second," the mayor groused, meaning anything but. "Tell her we're talking about a hole-in-the-ground kind of cave. What other kind is there?"

The 3000 and Ruth chewed that over a bit before the green bear restated Ruth's question. "She's wondering what the cave was made of."

Mayor Crawdaddy nearly fell off Twigs's back when he heard that one. I could see his point. The only thing I'd ever heard of caves being made from was rock, but I guess Twigs didn't know better. He took Ruth's question seriously, remembering backward with all his might.

"Rock," he finally said.

"Perfect," the mayor quipped. "Just perfect. If that's all the better you can do, we might as well call it quits right now."

Twigs got his back up about that and tried again, saying, "Hard rock."

"Like your head?" the mayor asked.

"No, smooth," Twigs said, without realizing he'd been insulted. "Smooth, hard rock."

That stumped all of us but good, not that Mayor Crawdaddy would ever admit such a thing.

"Is that the best you can do!" he blew up.

Twigs took the mayor's outburst to heart. Hoping to cheer him up a little, I gave him a scratch behind his furry ear and asked, "Can you remember anything else about the cave?"

The young woolly did his best, I'll give him that. He whimpered and shuffled his feet, but all he recalled were things that choked him up pretty bad. Things about his home, I'm guessing. He kept shaking his head and sniffling, saying to himself, "I can't go back there. Not anymore."

Listening to him made me wonder if he wasn't trying to cover up something. It seemed that the blizzard wasn't the only thing hiding things from us. I even got the idea that maybe Twigs was trying to conceal something from himself. What that could be, I hadn't a clue. I only recognized it as a possibility because I'd been known to try and pull the same stunt on myself from time to time. It sure seemed as if some naggy, guilty feelings had gotten under the big galumpus's skin, though he remembered something else before I could ask what he was holding back.

"A creek!" he blurted triumphantly. "Outside the cave was a creek."

"At least that's something we can work with," Mayor Crawdaddy reluctantly granted. "There's only one of those around here, though it's way on the other side of the park."

"That fits," the 3000 said. "He wandered a while before I caught up with him in that bog."

Just then an owl *who-who-who*-ed from down the hill behind us, except that it was an awful fakey *who-who-who*.

"That's no owl," the mayor declared.

"You may be correct," the 3000 agreed after she whirred and twisted her head around to hear better. "That does not match any owl recordings still intact in my databanks."

The mayor was right in the middle of sharing some snippy thoughts about databanks when the Earl of Sussex showed up in the branches above, making his usual grand entrance.

"Go!" he screeched. "Now! Fast!"

Normally I wasn't in the habit of following Sussex's advice, but I changed my mind when the saber-toothed tiger caveman staggered out from between a couple of nearby trees as if thrown. He kept his balance for two steps before falling to his knees. Sticky snow left him more snowman than caveman. His skimpy beard was turning into an icicle. After his dunking in the pond, his soaked animal skins would soon be frozen stiff as boards. We were snow-covered and camouflaged pretty good, too, but he looked much colder. The only one who looked warm was the 3000. Her body heat still melted any flakes landing on her and made her green fur glisten and stand out in the storm.

Righting himself, the caveman shook his spear at us as if hoping to scare us off.

One of the other cavemen shouted something from behind him.

"They're telling him to quit stalling," the 3000 reported.

Pointing the spear at us, the saber-tooth urged us to do something in a hushed whisper.

"And he's begging us to go away," the 3000 said, "before he has to do something he'd rather not."

"Like what?" Twigs sniffled.

None of us felt like speculating about that, though the 3000 did say, "Class, I suggest we keep moving."

Meanwhile the other cavemen went on shouting at the saber-toothed one. There wasn't time for the 3000 to translate what they were going on about, but it didn't sound flattering. Having heard the same belittling tone from Sussex a time or two, I figured they were calling him a coward, or worse. He did look flustered. Finally, he'd heard enough and angrily yelled something back at the others while poking the 3000 with his spear. That wasn't anywhere near what I'd call a smart move.

With her visual sensors busted, the 3000 couldn't see the attack, but when the spear glanced off her metal-and-plastic shoulder, she didn't have any trouble feeling it. She grabbed the pointy end of the spear and flung it back down the hill. The young caveman would have been fine if he'd let go of the spear, but he must have had some terrible kind of sentimental attachment to it. He acted terrified of what would happen if he lost it. Unwilling to give it up, he held on and went sailing away with the spear.

Just then the wolf-headed caveman roared into sight.

Grabbing a paw full of Twigs's fur, I yanked to get us moving. We pressed on. Four steps later we reached the top of the hill, skidded off the bike trail, and crashed downward, busting through brush, and over saplings, and off tree trunks. Sometimes I could see the Smokey 3000's green glow behind us, but other times it showed up ahead of us as we tumbled and twisted and rolled down that hill. Branches slapped us. Bark scraped us. Sussex shouted at us from somewhere nearby.

"Told you!"

There were plenty of yowls, mine and the mayor's.

"Is anyone steering?" yelled the 3000, still holding on to Twigs's tail.

Ruth shouted something from behind us. I got the idea she wanted us to go faster.

Twigs trumpeted. It was a lost, frightened sound, like something plugged and strangled and cornered all at once.

"If we get out of this in one piece—" the mayor threatened through clenched teeth.

There wasn't any need for him to finish his thought. I'd heard that threat often enough to know how it went.

"I'm fired," I finished for him.

That conversation took us to the bottom of the hill, where we hit a bump and went flying. Don't ask me how but Twigs thumped down feetfirst in the middle of the Theodore Wirth Parkway, a two-lane blacktop road

that hadn't been plowed yet. The mayor and I were still clinging to his back, breathing hard.

We'd barely gotten used to still being alive when a fierce scraping sound came roaring our way through the storm. It wasn't far enough away for my tastes and was closing in fast.

"What's that?" choked Crawdaddy.

I didn't get the idea that he really wanted to know. It sounded as though something was trying to tear the hide off the earth. At the same time, a smoldering golden cloud was mushrooming out of the darkness. And deep down the earth was rumbling, making it sound as though the cloud was escaping from underground. I half expected a cave to open up and a fire-breathing beast with a hundred heads and twice as many mouths to come climbing out it. I hadn't been expecting to find Twigs's cave so fast.

But wait a minute. Did any of this make sense? Not outside of a movie it didn't.

Whatever was bearing down on us sounded as though it was crunching the road to bits. It would probably pulverize us right along with it. I could only hope it'd spit us back out when it found out how gristly we were.

I can guarantee you that Twigs was trying to keep his eyes closed.

Ruth shouted some sort of warning.

"Mayday! Mayday!" broadcasted the Smokey 3000.

"Gilly!" barked the mayor. "Do something!"

Given the size of beast coming our way, I didn't think that anything I could do would help. But maybe Twigs was big enough to slow down whatever it was, if I could rouse him to do something. Wrenching my eyes away from the oncoming golden cloud, I scrambled over Twigs's head to his trunk, which I pinched with all my might. That brought him to life. With a start, he snapped his trunk and sent me flying straight at the cloud. That wasn't exactly the something I'd had in mind.

The next to last thing I saw was Twigs and Ruth scrambling into the woods on the far side of the road. At least they'd gotten away. I couldn't see the mayor but figured he was still clinging to the woolly's back. Where the 3000 had gotten to was anybody's guess. Her green glow wasn't in sight, and I didn't have time to search for her, although I suppose I should confess that I did find a spare moment to wish I was with the Earl of Sussex. No doubt that red squirrel had found somewhere safe to hang out. He usually did.

The golden cloud arrived! All of a sudden I had an idea what singed moths saw when they flew into a bright light. Tiny specks glowed and danced around me, sticking to my fur and whiskers. For a second I thought I was on fire! Then I realized the cloud was cold, not hot. The specks weren't embers but snowflakes. They reflected brilliant light everywhere.

I did some marveling.

That only lasted until my head cracked against something far solider than a snowflake. So much for all the gee-whiz sights. Whatever I bounced off felt like rock and landed me in a snowy ditch.

The last thing I saw? The red taillights of a truck rumbling off into the white night. How had it gotten mixed up in all this? Then it dawned on me. The smoldering golden cloud? It was a huge wave of snow kicked up by a snowplow and lit by the truck's flashing yellow roof lights. The rock I'd bounced off? The truck's windshield.

After that came enough darkness to fill my head with night.

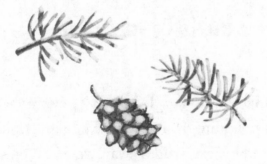

Chapter 15

Puddle-dunked

Toenail to eyelash, I tingled everywhere. My heart was pounding in my ears. The faint tinkling of glass reached me from miles away, where I'd once fallen off a roof while batting at wind chimes. Their sound drifted my way whenever something life-threatening happened.

My nose twitched as though someone was holding a burnt stick beneath it. The all-too-familiar smell of woodsmoke mixed with charcoal rushed my way. I traced that back to a sooty hot dog I'd once snagged out of a smoldering campfire that had almost set me ablaze. Adding to the perfumery was something rather minty, as if I'd landed on top of a patch of catnip that was buried beneath the snow. No time to figure that out, though.

A drifty, drowsy feeling swept over me. The treetops seemed close by, though I couldn't exactly see them. I couldn't see anything but a glossy, moonlit fog that pooled around me.

It was the same fog I saw every time I played dead.

Out of the fog stepped my ma, carrying me and a whole passel of my brothers and sisters on her back. It was one crowded ride, and full of remember-when-we-used-to questions: Remember when we used to raid that strawberry patch on starry nights? Remember when we sent that floppy-eared rabbit packing? Remember when we laughed at Cousin Oprah for wanting to be a butterfly so that she could fly away from trouble instead of playing dead?

I was having myself a vision—playing dead often brought them on.

But it wasn't only my family sitting on Ma's back—the Smokey 3000, all green and glowy, was riding along too. How could she fit on my mother's back? She couldn't, except in a vision. Who knows why she was in the mix, but now I was stuck with trying to figure out what she stood for.

I'm sorry to say it, but visions can be awfully big on warnings, omens, and gloomy forecasts. And drat the luck, this one wasn't any different. I could see the 3000's mouth moving up and down, as if trying to warn me of something, though I couldn't hear a single word she was saying. That was sort of normal. My visions generally prefer to leave things up to my imagination and don't give me any rest until I figure out their meaning.

So I worked up a considerable sweat concentrating on what the 3000 was trying to tell me. Eventually I did manage to catch one word she was passing on.

"Don't."

Now, wasn't that just typical?

Don't what?

Along with all my other worries and regrets I was now going to have to squeeze in figuring out a *don't*.

To make matters even more fun, I started hearing another voice, one from outside my vision. It sounded far away and harsher than the 3000's, maybe because it was so grumbly and put out and on the lookout for someone to blame for all his troubles. The Honorable Mayor Crawdaddy on his high horse came to mind, except that this voice was human, which meant that I didn't understand a word of what he was saying, only its tone.

Whoever was talking was also nudging me, testing to see if I was alive. It was a rough kind of poke. That was good. It meant that the poker didn't want to get any too close to me. And that was the plan—when playing dead, I twisted up horribly on my back, and pulled my gums back to show my sharp teeth, and did my level best to smell . . . dead. The general idea was that anybody with a lick of sense wouldn't want to bother with me.

Another human, a man, rumbled something from a

couple steps farther away. He sounded plenty outraged and disgusted about what was going on.

What's this miserable thing? His tone seemed to be saying.

I couldn't be sure, what with my eyes squinty closed and all, but I had a strong hunch that the *miserable* thing he was talking about was me.

I knew I should have stayed home was another thing his disgusted tone could have been saying.

Just leave him was a third possibility.

Naturally I was rooting for the third possibility. But whatever he was saying, his tone definitely didn't make me want to pop up and introduce myself. Maybe that was what the 3000 in my vision had been trying to tell me. *Don't* as in *Don't get up.*

Then another voice spoke, and this one sounded kind of hopeful, which I didn't take as a good sign at all.

Think he might be good to eat? This voice seemed to be asking.

When you're playing dead and dare not peek, it's awful easy to imagine that the horriblest, baddest, unluckiest sorts of things are being said.

Looks like some kind of overgrown rat, the second voice's tone said.

Insulting things were sure to come to me too.

If I have to eat another rat, the third voice's tone complained, *I might sprout a tail.*

Me too, agreed the second voice's tone.

Or was it the first voice's tone? It can be awful hard to keep track when I was all curled up and my head was upside down and I was halfway stuck in a vision. Behind my mostly closed eyes a part of me was still riding around on my ma's back with all my brothers and sisters. They were lobbing insults at the voices above us, as well as at the 3000, who went on dishing up *Don't*s.

"Nobody asked you!" my brother Lebron shouted in my vision.

"You should be so lucky," added my sister Selena, meaning the men should be so lucky as to have a tail.

"Scat!" screamed two or three of my brothers and sisters at once.

I was almost surprised the men couldn't hear them, full-throated as they were carrying on.

Then one of the men standing above me bellowed

something at the top of his lungs. Everyone inside and outside my vision quieted.

Enough! his tone seemed to say to the other two voices. *The whole world knows you're hungry, but going on and on about it ain't going to fill our bellies any sooner. You need to do what I tell you! That's the only way we're ever going to get out of this flea-infested land.*

That may seem like a lot to get from just somebody's tone, but I've been playing dead for quite a while and have reading people's tones down to something of a science. I'm not saying that I have every little detail of what the guy was saying exactly right, but I'm pretty sure I nailed the general spirit of what he was getting at.

I was so sure that I got a little mad about it. Flea-infested land, my foot! If anyone had bothered to ask me, I'd have told them that nobody likes a complainer. By then I was thinking it was the three cavemen who had me surrounded. That explained the minty smell that was haunting my nose. Ten thousand years ago, when they'd first started stalking Twigs, they must have tried to hide their scent from him by rubbing mint all over themselves. Tricky. But forget how sweet they smelled. Whoever was standing over me was acting ornery as a puddle-dunked groundhog. All of which made me put off introducing myself a while longer.

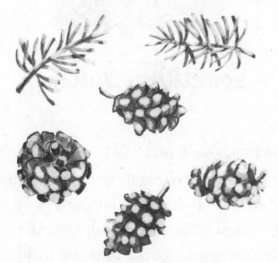

Chapter 16

Something Yummy

Too bad I couldn't put off introducing myself forever, but their angry voices put an end to my vision. My
ma waddled off into one of the lingering patches of fog,
carrying the rest of my family with her. All my brothers and sisters waved goodbye while reminding me that
I never should have taken up with Mayor Crawdaddy.
Loneliness descended. The Smokey 3000 was still riding on Ma's back, too, and the green bear mouthed
Don't one last time as I watched them go. When they

were gone, I sneaked a peek at the real world, hoping for a glimpse of what I was up against.

The voices had stepped away from me for a minute to go after each other, so it seemed like a safe time to check things out. Just as I'd thought, it was those cavemen, standing in the middle of the freshly plowed road.

The loudest, meanest voice belonged to Boar-head, who was ripping into Saber-tooth for all he was worth.

Pitiful! Boar-head's tone said. *Don't embarrass me. I know what's best!*

Saber-tooth sputtered back in a sulky, poor-me kind of way, *But, Pa.* It sure sounded as though Theodore Wirth Park was the last place he wanted to be. Maybe finding himself in the belly of some beast would have ranked lower, but not by much.

At which point Boar-head cranked it up another notch and boomed away, his tone saying, *Stop right there. I don't want to hear one more "But, Pa" coming out of your yap. NOT ONE! Your mother and I have done everything we could to get you started right in life, but if you—*

To which Saber-tooth answered dejectedly, *Yes, Pa.*

And then old Wolf-head piled on, sounding as though he was lecturing Saber-tooth about ground they'd covered many a time before.

You young pup, Wolf-head's tone said. *You ought to be grateful for everything your pa's given you. Back when I was your age, I didn't have anything but a rock to my name, and it wasn't any kind of smooth rock either. It was chipped and cracked and heavy to lug around. And I can tell you . . .*

Saber-tooth rolled his eyes and kept his head down.

Things were getting interesting. Unable to help myself, I kept right on peeking, probably more than I should have. I was hoping to spot an opening to make a getaway into the blizzard, which wouldn't you know was coming down heavier than ever.

Hey! Boar-head shouted something that sounded awful eager to change the subject. He was looking right at me as he yelled it, too.

Oops. I guess maybe I got a little carried away with my peeking. Of course, I slammed my eyes shut as fast as I could. But too late. Someone jerked me off the ground and dangled me upside down. It must have been Boar-head who was yakking at me now. He didn't seem to be saying anything flattering or friendly, and he wasn't the slightest bit wishy-washy about it either.

Hey, you! he seemed to shout. *Unless you want a good bashing with my meat maker, open your eyes.*

Or something like that. He didn't need to ask twice. My eyes popped open—I couldn't have kept them closed on a dare.

Boar-head was holding me by the tail while shaking his club at me, the same club that had flattened the 3000's hat and knocked out her vision and black-eyed Susie and databanks. He had a red smear down the bridge of his nose and slashes of the same red under his eyes. Proud as he was acting, you'd have thought he'd slayed a scaly monster instead of tripped over some poor possum who was playing dead. Spittle flew off his cracked lips when he spoke. His eyes glared through a tangle of hair and beard like a couple of torches lost in a dark forest.

The other two cavemen were almost as colorful. Wolf-head went in for orange dots of mud all over his face and wore a necklace of dried roots that looked like shrunken fingers and toes. Old as he was, his snarl of hair and beard were a yellowed white, and he'd mis-placed all his teeth but one, which had a serious wobble to it, as if about to go missing any day now. A small turtle shell that was painted yellow dangled off his deer-hide belt. Every once in a while he gave that shell a shake. Something like rocks rattled inside it and made him cackle as if they gave him secret powers.

Saber-tooth was by far the youngest and runtiest of the bunch. To make up for that he'd gobbed green and blue mud all over his forehead and nose and peach-fuzzy cheeks. His necklace wasn't anything but a couple of cracked clamshells. Shivering beneath his soaked robe, he kept his head down as if about to apologize for something. He acted resentful about having to do it.

They were all sniffing my way and smacking their lips and rubbing their tummies as if looking forward to filling them with something yummy—something like me. It was enough to make me play dead all over again. I could feel the fogbank rolling back in, though nowhere near fast enough to suit me.

Saber-tooth was mumbling something contrary. *Doesn't look so tasty to me!*

Wolf-head leaned toward the practical *We'll have to cook him to find out.*

And Boar-head treated them both like dummies. *Cook him? There's not enough of him to bother with cooking. Let's just chop him up and throw him down as is.*

None of which left me feeling overly confident about my future. I surely never thought I'd end up in the middle of Theodore Wirth Parkway hoping that three cavemen would take the time to cook me. I guess it goes without saying that Mayor Crawdaddy was nowhere in sight. Sussex was long gone too. Not about to go down without a fight, I was fixing to throw my weight into swinging sideways toward Boar-head's arm so that I could give it a nip, but something chirped from a nearby snowbank before I could sink my teeth into anything.

We all heard it.

The cavemen crouched and spun toward the new sound as if some big slobbery beast had called out their names. It didn't sound that scary to me, barely more than a cranky cricket, but those three cavemen were awfully jumpy after that snowplow had thundered past.

Boar-head snapped at Wolf-head, who yelled at Saber-tooth and tried to push him toward the chirp. Saber-tooth had other ideas and stayed put, shouting something that could only have meant *You go!*

Whatever was chirping in that snowbank, none of those cavemen wanted anything to do with it.

In the end, Wolf-head disgustedly quit egging on Saber-tooth and advanced toward the chirping on his own. He moved with mincing little steps, mumbling to himself all the way. With one hand, he held his spear. The other gripped a gnarly, shriveled root that was part of his necklace. The way he kept the root out in front of himself and whispered real hush-hush to it, even kissing it once or twice, he must have been expecting big things from it. He didn't seem to think that hooves, horns, and chompers were anything to worry about, not so long as he had that root protecting him.

Boar-head rode him pretty rough, hoping to put some pep into the old man's steps, but Wolf-head wasn't about to be hurried. He stopped often, cocking his head to listen to whatever was going on inside the snowbank. He took so long to cross the road that the chirping got fainter, simmered down into a raspy whir, and finally dropped away completely. Relieved, Wolf-head kissed that root one more time, right before giving the others a modest shrug that said, *There. It's gone. Anything else you want me and this root to take care of?*

Keep going. Boar-head jabbed his club at the snowbank and grunted, sharp-like.

Wolf-head broke out a whole new batch of muttering

before creeping forward again. Upon reaching the snow-bank, he had one last word with the root on his necklace before gripping his spear with both hands.

Real careful-like, he poked the snowbank a half dozen times or so. Whatever was in there, he was doing his best not to wake it up or make it mad.

Boar-head shared some disparaging thoughts about how long it was taking. *Afraid of a little snow?* his tone said. *You're worse than Saber-tooth. Am I going to have to come over there and show you how to do it?*

With a growl, Wolf-head jabbed his spear into the snowbank as deep as he could. He really threw his weight into it. He shouted, too.

Take that!

His spear sank into the bank a good three feet before clunking into something solid. Whatever he'd struck didn't sound anything like snow. Matter of fact, I don't think I'd ever heard anything that sounded less like snow. When he tried tugging his spear back out, it stayed stuck no matter how hard he yanked.

The chirping came back too. Louder, angrier.

Dropping me and gripping his club with both

hands, Boar-head barked at Saber-tooth. He must have told him to help the old man, but the youngster did just the opposite and backed away. He'd barely taken a step before a yowl from Wolf-head stopped him cold.

Whatever was chirping had jerked the spear away from Wolf-head, making him stagger backward and land on his rump.

A green, furry arm shot out of the snowbank. Its paw was holding on to Wolf-head's spear, which it flung toward the woods we'd just tumbled out of.

Scrambling to his feet, Wolf-head pushed past Saber-tooth. For an old guy, he had some lively legs. They all tore off straight down the plowed road, which was the fastest way out of there. Boar-head was leading the way. In nothing flat I couldn't see a bit of their flapping robes or catch a whiff of mint as they raced into the blizzard.

Chapter 17

A Bionic Harmonizer

The 3000 sat up, brushed off some snow, and asked a question in several different languages before finding one that made sense to me.

"Class? Is anyone there?" the 3000 asked in North American Animal Speech.

I was standing right next to her, so apparently she was still blind.

"I'm here," I answered.

"The possum named Gilly?" the 3000 asked after

some whirring and clicking that went on deep inside her. "Can you see the cavemen?"

"They skedaddled," I told her. "Ran off as fast as they could go. Are you all right?"

"Why, thank you for asking," the 3000 politely answered. "A systems check shows me functioning at fifty-six percent of capacity."

"Is that good?"

"My specs list it as falling outside an acceptable range for operation and advises maintenance as soon as possible."

I'd never been around a robot before, not in person anyway, and I'd only seen them on TV a few times, but this one sure had a nice set of manners. She reminded me of my aunty J Lo, who never had a bad thing to say about anybody and had been known to stand up to coyotes.

"You were chirping pretty good," I pointed out.

"My bionic harmonizer is out of sync."

"Mine's been acting up a little too," I said.

Her head swiveled my way and there was a pause, as she considered what I'd said.

"You're making a joke?" she asked.

"It's been known to happen," I admitted, though as a general rule few enough noticed. The 3000 went up another notch in my estimation.

But poking fun at a robot's bionic harmonizer left me feeling kind of shabby. Hadn't this green bear just saved me from a cooking pot? She had. Shouldn't that ought to count for something? It should. An apology seemed in order.

"Sorry for making fun of you."

I halfway expected her to remind me that robots didn't have feelings. At least in movies they never seemed to. But maybe they built their robots different ten thousand or so years from now. Maybe they'd figured out how to pack pride and anger and love inside the 3000 before covering her with green fur.

"Thank you for thinking I might have feelings," she said. "I can see why Mayor Crawdaddy picked you as an assistant."

"You can?"

"You've traits he's lacking."

"Most anyone would."

"Are you joking again?" she asked.

"Not that I know of. Are you able to stand?"

She buzzed a bit. "Just a moment, please. My gyroscopic sensor is realigning itself." Something clinked inside her. "There."

Lifting her arms straight in front of herself for balance, she slowly rose to her feet and did a deepknee bend.

"I'm checking my calibrations," she told me.

"Good idea," I answered, wondering what she was talking about. Sometimes it just feels right to say something.

Halfway down, the 3000 got stuck. Something inside her hummed loudly, then cut out. Her green fur winked off, went dark. Her arms stayed stretched out in front of her, locked in place.

It occurred to me that I was in a real pickle if that robot couldn't pull herself together.

The woods silently spread out all around us. The lightning and thunder went on, although for the moment farther away. Somewhere out there the cavemen were probably regrouping. Everything about the city surrounding our park was rubbed out by the blizzard. For once I wouldn't have minded having the Earl of Sussex on hand, just to hear him prattle.

I was about to ask the 3000 how she was doing but before I could . . .

"Uncle Fester!"

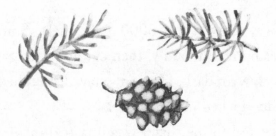

Chapter 18

Tusks

Ruth scooped me up and hugged me so tight I nearly popped. Then she cradled me, and baby-talked to me, and tickled my snowy whiskers as if afraid she'd lost me forever. *Uncle Fester,* said her tone, *don't scare me that way.* If the mayor or Sussex had been around, they'd have never let me live it down.

After a bit she spoke to the 3000, who didn't answer. In fact, a little snow had started sticking to the green bear's shoulders and hat brim, along with her furry forearms, too, which made it seem as if nobody was at home. Still holding me, Ruth shook the 3000's shoulder with her free hand. With a shudder, the robot came back to life—green glow, humming bionic harmonizer, clicking gyroscopics, and all.

"Class," the 3000 announced, "I am back online."

The robot and Ruth talked until the 3000 said to me, "Twigs and Mayor Crawdaddy are up ahead. Twigs has hurt his leg and is moving slowly. That's why Ruth came back without them."

"Is that all?" I asked, thinking that they'd talked longer than that little bit.

"She wanted me to make sure you hadn't broken anything. I told her that I'd run a complete diagnostic and you are fine."

"Anything else?" I said, charmed that Ruth was worried about me.

"There was some confusion over your name," the 3000 said. "I thought you were Gilly?"

"That's right," I said. "Short for Gilligan."

The 3000 considered that a moment before asking, "From the classic TV show?"

"Exactly," I said, impressed by how smart that robot was.

"Somehow she thinks your name is Uncle Fester."

"I've noticed. Search me why. I'm Gilly."

When the 3000 filled Ruth in on her mistake, she apologized to me in what sounded like ten different ways, until her face was red, and according to the 3000, she promised to get my name right from that moment on.

"Tell her it's no big deal," I said. "Is that all the two of you were going on about?"

"She did want you to promise to leave snowplows alone."

"Deal. That all?"

"She mentioned that her family's probably worried about her."

"I'm sure they are."

"And that someday she hopes to be a veterinarian."

"I'm sure she'll make a good one," I said, "but why'd she bring up something like that?"

"I think she might be worried about not getting a chance to grow up and do it."

"Why wouldn't she?"

"The blizzard and sharp spears and time traveling might get in her way."

"Oh. Will you tell her that I'll protect her?"

When the 3000 passed that on, Ruth hugged me all over again.

"Anything else?" I asked, once able to breathe.

"She did ask if I thought we'd reach the time tunnel in time."

"What'd you tell her?"

"That the longer we stood around talking about it, the poorer our chances."

"Right. Let's get moving."

To make better time, Ruth tucked me into her backpack and we were off, following Twigs's trail, which was quickly filling up with snow. I put up with riding there for Twigs's sake. The extra mittens and a tasseled stocking cap cushioning my ride didn't have anything to do with it, though it was cozy as my mother's pouch in there, which did help revive my spirits. There were granola bars, too, though I'd sort of lost my appetite after having those cavemen smack their lips over me. Sticking my pink nose out the top of the pack, I took in the view.

Trailing behind us, the 3000 was hanging on to a strap attached to Ruth's backpack. Snowflakes were once again melting on her green fur, making her glisten.

We'd left the road and were trooping through the woods that stretched away from the quaking bog. The trees we passed were masked by the snow plastered to their trunks and weighing down their boughs. The only noise was the crunch of Ruth's and the 3000's feet on snow, but that was so loud that it sounded as if the whole woods was on the march with us.

"They shouldn't be far," the 3000 reported when I asked for an update.

From Ruth's backpack I couldn't see the drifts piled up ahead of us, only the ones Twigs had already plowed through. The big galumpus was headed in the general direction of the creek, but meandering, which must have meant the mayor was navigating. That raccoon didn't have any better sense of direction than a twiddlebug.

"What were those cavemen talking about?" I asked the 3000 as we bumped along.

"Tusks."

"Tusks?" I said, surprised. Here I'd been thinking

they were only going on about cooking yours truly. A little peeved, I asked, "What kind of tusks?"

"Woolly mammoth tusks. The youngest one, the one wearing the saber-tooth skin, needs to collect a pair of them to prove he's an adult. That is why they're tracking Twigs."

"Now, just a minute!" I squirmed halfway out of Ruth's backpack. "Does Twigs know that?"

"Class, I believe we can safely assume he does," the 3000 answered. "His herd would have been hunted regularly by cavemen."

"So what are we going to do about it?"

"Try to get him back to his herd. That's where he'll be safest."

"And if they catch up to us again before we get him there?"

"It'd be best if we didn't let that happen," the 3000 said. "I'm sorry to report that my defensive capacities are diminished."

"What are you trying to say?"

"That I may not be much help if we have to fight them off again."

I was about to ask how much help she might not be when the cavemen started *a-woo*ing behind us. Their voices faded in and out as the wind shifted.

"Gilly," Ruth scolded, along with a bunch of other words that sounded worried and almost cross.

Gilly, what have you got me into? she might have been saying. Or, *Gilly, I'm going as fast as I can.* Or just, *Gilly, this is bad. Real bad.* I almost missed hearing her call me Uncle Fester.

"She's worrying about what Twigs might run into up ahead," the 3000 passed on.

"Are you sure?" I asked, wondering if the 3000's translation program might be failing. It sure didn't sound to me as if Ruth was fussing about Twigs.

"Positive."

Well, I wasn't going to argue with her about what Ruth was trying to tell me. I reckoned the 3000 was doing the best she could while teetering along behind us. Still, she didn't seem to be glowing as bright as before meeting up with that snowplow, and a couple of times I could have sworn I saw her fur flicker longer than ever.

"How are you doing?" I asked her.

"System deterioration continues," the 3000 answered, "though at the moment I'm more concerned about what's behind us than my condition."

"You mean the cavemen?"

"I do."

"Can you hear where they are?"

"Oh yes, class. They're approximately one hundred yards back, determined as ever to collect some tusks."

"Do you think there's any chance of talking them out of that?" I asked.

"None whatsoever. Once humans get their minds set on something, it's nearly impossible to reason with them."

"Maybe we could offer them something else," I suggested.

"I don't believe it would help. This group seems particularly single-minded in their quest. Remember, that boy's trying to prove he's ready to be a grown-up. That's an extremely important event to them, and so far as they are concerned, there's only one way he can do it—by collecting a pair of tusks."

"He doesn't seem too eager," I pointed out.

"I concur," the 3000 agreed, "but I'm afraid his elders will convince him he has no choice."

"Well, it's dumb. My mother never sent me after tusks to prove anything."

"Perhaps not, but from their view, sending him after a woolly mammoth makes a great deal of sense. Acquiring a pair of tusks requires bravery, which makes it an excellent test of adulthood."

"Gilly," Ruth shushed.

She held her hand up as if she'd heard something. A moment later I heard it, too, some kind of honk. I supposed it could have been a car horn, but bumpy as this outing had been so far, it seemed more likely it was Twigs, in trouble.

Ruth seemed to agree. With a shout, she took off running.

Hold on! her tone said.

Rushing toward trouble was new territory for a possum, so I might have squeaked in surprise, just a little—a few excited words to let Ruth know that I was still with her.

A couple of minutes later, what was left of Twigs's

trail left the park and entered a backyard. Fences didn't wall off the park on the east side, and Twigs's tracks passed between two houses before turning onto a city street. At least Crawdaddy got that much right. The street he'd picked angled toward an arm of the park that Bassett Creek ran through.

The lights on that side of Theodore Wirth were working. House windows bloomed like daisies in the night. Nothing had been plowed. Smooth white mounds lined both sides of the street. Parked cars, I assumed. Though considering what had already stepped out of this storm, I didn't want to jump to any hasty conclusions. Twice we passed snowmen whose fierce black eyes tracked us as if we were thieves.

Why did the mayor have Twigs marching straight down the center of the street? What if a car or truck came gunning out of nowhere?

The sound of breaking glass saved me from overthinking that worry. Ruth heard it, too, and stopped in her tracks. The noise came from behind us, so I guessed the cavemen had reached the houses and met up with a window. One of them yelped in surprise. Most likely they didn't have windows ten thousand years back. It sounded like the wolf-headed one was doing the yelling.

"He's telling the others that the house is warm inside," the 3000 relayed to me. She must have passed the same news on to Ruth, for we started racing forward again.

The cavemen's delighted whoops faded behind us, but up ahead Twigs went right on squalling away as if he'd met up with a field of octopuses or stack of camels or the Earl of Sussex's worst nightmare—a yard full of chipmunks. He sounded all wound up about it. I was pretty sure that if he was a possum, he'd be playing dead.

Then the whir of a motor reached us. Not only that, but it started growing louder too. Ruth raised her voice to call out to the big galumpus, though I doubt he heard her above the racket.

We dashed onward until nearly rear-ending Twigs, who'd come to a complete stop in the middle of the street. Even a blizzard couldn't hide a backside that size.

The young woolly was swaying his head from side to side as if he couldn't believe what he was hearing. His trunk was lifted high and blatting. He also spared a moment or two to whimper about his left front foot, which he was raising and lowering as if it hurt to put any weight on it.

Mayor Crawdaddy was scrunched down on Twigs's shoulder, wearing a coat of white and looking as happy as a plucked duck.

"What's that sound?" I called out.

"Nothing good," Crawdaddy snapped. "And it's headed our way."

"Class," the 3000 said, "we appear to have an internal combustion engine approaching. Please don't be disappointed, but corrupted memory prevents me from determining an exact match. However, I do believe it to be a model common to the twentieth and twenty-first centuries."

"Let's at least get off the street," I urged.

"Can't," the mayor said with disgust. "Your big friend here claims to have hurt his foot and won't budge."

While the mayor filled me in on how Twigs had somehow stepped into a storm drain, Ruth and the 3000 sorted out our next move.

"Settle down, class," the 3000 said once they had

finished talking. "Ruth has volunteered to check out what is coming our way."

Don't assume that satisfied the mayor. He went right on harping about Twigs's clumsiness. Fortunately, that didn't slow Ruth down. First, she positioned the 3000 so that the bear could hold on to Twigs's tail and wouldn't get left behind if we had to take off. That done, she stepped around the woolly in snow nearly up to her waist. Halfway past him, she paused to toss me onto Twigs's back alongside the mayor, who still hadn't shut up about our guest's shortcomings.

"This galumpus is moving slower than creeping jenny," the mayor complained. "I think he might be part possum. And I'll tell you something else, too: if I'd have known that I was going to have to handle this mess all by myself—"

The rest of his bellyaching got drowned out by a rumble that was closing fast.

Chapter 19

Free Advice

Ruth yelled from up ahead, where she'd disappeared into the storm. It sounded as though she was
trying to get someone's attention, but the roar of the
approaching motor covered up most of what she said.

"I'm putting you in charge of all future catastrophes,"
the mayor grumbled in my ear.

I'd heard that bluff before, usually when the mayor
ran into something he didn't want to touch.

"What's a catastrophe?" Twigs asked from beneath us.

"You," the mayor snapped.

"I am?" Twigs said, impressed. "I never knew that. Is that good?"

"Don't worry about it." I patted Twigs on the back. "We're all catastrophes at one time or another."

"We are?"

"Yes," I assured him. "We are. How's your leg?"

"I think I might have broke it."

That sounded far-fetched, considering that he'd been managing to walk on it.

"Can you bend it?" I asked.

"Not so much," the big galumpus quavered. Turning hopeful, he added, "Maybe you'll have to let me stay here with you."

"We've been over that," the mayor growled.

"It's not safe for you here," I reminded Twigs, speaking up to be heard above the motor coming our way.

"Why not?" Twigs asked, turning willful.

"Cavemen," I said.

"That green bear can protect me from them."

"Class," the 3000 chimed in, cranking up her voice another notch to be heard, "I'm sorry to report that the blow to my head has short-circuited several of my major systems, creating a power drain that has taken my Newtonian force beam offline."

"You and them excuses," the mayor crossly fussed.

"I'm not offering an excuse, class. I'm giving you an assessment of the realities facing us. Compounding my system failures is the fact that it is night, to say nothing of being totally overcast, which means that my solar collectors have been unable to recharge my batteries since arriving here."

"Oh, please," the mayor bad-mouthed, "don't think that I haven't heard that one before."

So far as I knew, no one in all the recorded history of Theodore Wirth Park had ever heard that one before. If I hadn't had to shout to be heard, I might have called the old fraud out on it.

"Class," the 3000 cautioned, "manners, please."

Meanwhile, the motor kept getting closer, clunking and churning and sounding as though fueled by broken glass and smashed cans. A single white eye came smoking and burning through the storm. Naturally it was headed straight at us. Was there any other direction that Trouble could have gone? I had to shield my face against the glare and couldn't avoid thinking that maybe Ruth was right—she might never get a chance to become a veterinarian.

"What now?" the mayor bellyached at the top of his lungs.

"A-gosh," squeaked Twigs, sounding mouse-sized.

If I squinted, I could barely make out the edges of a human contraption taking shape behind the white eye. I could also see Ruth's outline between us and it. Holding her ground, Ruth raised a hand to signal for the thing to stop.

I tried telling her that might not be a great idea, unless she was secretly some kind of superhero like the ones always showing up in movies. She couldn't hear me above the engine, though, and even if she could have, she wouldn't have understood me without help from the 3000. And just then the 3000 was flickering, not translating.

While all that was going on, Mayor Crawdaddy made himself as small as a mustard seed and quietly slipped behind me.

Not having anywhere to hide, Twigs raised his trunk and trumpeted. If he was aiming to come across as brave, he missed by a considerable distance. A squeeze toy on its last legs would have sounded more courageous.

"Don't you come any closer," the big galumpus warned, "or I'll make you go away. I mean it!"

He must have been hoping that his wisher was working better than the last time he'd tried using it.

Wherever the Earl of Sussex had stashed himself, I wouldn't have minded joining him. At the moment I was catching a full whiff of woodsmoke and hearing a clash of wind chimes. But if I played dead, who was going to help Twigs? So I did my best to tough it out. When I finally managed to open my eyes, which had somehow or other gotten closed, the loudmouthed beast was still bearing down on us, but at least I wasn't riding on my mother's back with all my brothers and sisters, so maybe I'd dodged another vision.

The contraption headed our way looked and

sounded like something that escaped from a factory that made gadgets for movie villains. It roared, it belched, it smoked. It looked as though it was trying to gulp down the entire blizzard—snow, street, buried cars, and all.

Up went my hackles. Twigs cut loose with another toot, a mournful, lost, last-ditch cry for help. Even my cousin Bullwinkle couldn't have matched him for pitiful, and that sad sack had a knack for finding himself in the most bothersome kinds of trouble. I might have joined Twigs myself if I hadn't already figured out what was headed our way.

Any animal who foraged outside the park would have recognized it, but there's a considerable difference between sitting safely in a tree while watching one of those things tackle a snowdrift and finding one of them chomping your way all breathy and bright. From up close I could see that its mouth was full of spinning blades. Its breath was foul as bus fumes. Its eye smoked in the falling snow like one of those fire-breathing dragons in the movies Ruth sometimes watched. It was a snowblower, of course.

But it was the creature pushing the blower who

caught my eye. As he came slowly into view, I had myself a good long shiver, along with another dose of woodsmoke and wind chimes.

The creature behind the blower had an old bald head that was milkweed green and shaped like a leaky football. The rest of him stuck with the milkweed green, except for his eyes. Baby blue there. His ears were shaped like seedpods that had cracked open and sprouted tufts of white hair. The green hands holding the snowblower's handles had three sturdy claws, and he wore a belted white bathrobe. Thoughtful as his expression was, he looked as though he'd just woken up and was trying to remember a dream that kept getting away from him.

But strangest of all—I recognized him. He was straight out of a movie that Ruth's brother loved to watch. In it, the same creature in a white bathrobe flew around in spaceships, when he wasn't leaning on a cane and giving out free advice to a wide range of creatures, none of which lived in our park. He never had many takers for the advice, which left him sad and more than a little grumpy.

What was up with this blizzard? Was it strong enough to blow characters out of movies and set them loose on the streets? Why not? It'd already sent us a woolly mammoth, an educational robot, and three cavemen.

"Do something!" the mayor shouted in my ear.

"Class." The 3000 raised her voice. "What is happening?"

"There's a snowblower headed our way," I yelled over my shoulder.

"Pushed by a movie star," the mayor added.

So maybe Mayor Crawdaddy had seen a movie or two more than he liked to let on.

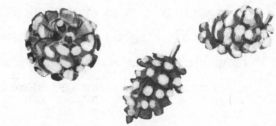

Chapter 20

Birdy

And then something even more unexpected than all the other unexpectedness happened. Ruth shouted and waved at the green creature, who shut off the snow-blower to hear. The silence that fell on us made me want to laugh in relief. But what happened after that stole the laugh away. First the creature answered Ruth in some language that she didn't seem to know. They went back and forth, getting more and more frustrated, until the creature reached his three-clawed hands up to his green head and slowly lifted it.

What kind of creature lifts his head off to greet you? It felt as if the inside of that green head might be completely empty, or worse, that it might be filled with every star in the sky, or a potted petunia, or a popcorn popper that was overflowing. Anything and everything seemed possible, except for what happened when the head lifted clear away.

It turned out to be a mask! Beneath it was a human head. That meant I'd been fooled the same way twice in one day. First by those cavemen, and now by this snowblower operator. If every rock hadn't been covered by snow, I'd have hunted one up to crawl under.

And that's not all. It turned out that I knew the guy.

Beneath the green bald-headed mask was another bald head that had a good-natured face and wore round eyeglasses. Everybody in the park knew and trusted this guy. He had a way of talking to himself that put everyone at ease. And it didn't matter how gnarly or matted you were, he treated you like a neighbor. We called him

Birdy on account of all the bird feeders he hung off his back deck.

I myself had spent many a lovely evening stretched out in one of Birdy's trees, nibbling on sunflower seeds he'd thoughtfully provided and enjoying his gigantic TV, which he always kept pointed toward a large picture window at the back of his house. So long as you didn't mind movies about spaceships and ray guns and robots—those were all that Birdy ever played—you'd have a great old time.

Ruth spoke again, sounding as if asking for help. Birdy answered, making far more sense to Ruth without the green mask muffling his words.

After listening to Ruth and Birdy talk a minute, the 3000 reported that Birdy was wearing a costume from a famous science fiction movie called *Star Wars*. He was dressed as a character called Yoda.

"What's a movie?" Twigs wanted to know.

Being from ten thousand years ago, he hadn't a clue, but the 3000 got him squared away on that quick as could be and also on why someone would want to dress up like a character named Yoda.

"To pretend he's someone he's not," the 3000 explained.

"Now, why would he want to do that?" Twigs asked, sounding a little too perplexed if you ask me. Something told me that the big galumpus knew more about such pretending than he was letting on.

"An excellent question," the 3000 complimented. "Class, would anyone care to answer?"

"Hold on now," the mayor said, feigning surprise. "Don't tell me we've run into a question you don't know the answer to?"

"Not at all," the 3000 answered. "But my subroutines have identified this as a teaching moment."

"Maybe he's pretending to be someone better than himself," I answered before the mayor could turn it into his own kind of moment.

"Would that work?" Twigs sounded doubtful, as if he knew someone who'd tried doing the same kind of pretending without any luck, someone who had trouble hiding due to his size, his tusks, and his trunk.

"Maybe he's trying to avoid facing himself," the mayor threw out.

"Oh." Twigs spoke as if he'd been discovered.

"Maybe he wants to make new friends," I suggested, hoping to steer Twigs away from dwelling on his own troubles.

"By being green?" Twigs asked, not seeing how that'd work.

"Perhaps," the 3000 said. "This one also says he's dressed up that way to stay warm."

"That makes sense," Twigs said, relieved to find something that did.

"Additionally," the 3000 went on, "there's another reason he's pushing the snowblower down the middle of the street in such a storm."

"There is?"

"He's checking on an elderly neighbor. He wants to make sure she's all right. Does anyone know what that means?"

"We shouldn't be scared of him?" Twigs guessed.

"That is exactly right," the 3000 said. "He's doing a good deed, which is excellent news for us."

"Since when?" the mayor asked.

"Tut, tut," the 3000 chided. "Since we found ourselves

in need of help. If this man goes around helping elderly neighbors, he might be willing to help us, too."

The mayor sourly mouthed the words *tut, tut* at me as if he'd never heard them before, but for once he kept the rest of his thoughts mostly to himself. Twigs shared, though.

"You mean he might let me stay with him?" the big galumpus said, inspired.

"Now, don't you think that sounds a little silly?" the 3000 asked. "A woolly mammoth living with a human?"

"Uh-uh," Twigs said, turning all earnest. "There was an old woolly who left our herd to live with a beaver down by the creek."

"What's that got to do with you and this human?" the mayor asked.

"Just saying," Twigs lamely answered.

"What about your family?" I asked, figuring it was time to change the topic.

"They wouldn't miss me."

"Now, I'm sure that's not true," I said.

"You don't know woolly mammoths," Twigs spitefully answered.

He had a point there.

"Staying with this human would never work," the 3000 said.

"Why not?"

"Time contamination."

"So?"

"That's not good. You don't want to pollute current events with earlier or later ones."

"Says who?"

They argued back and forth about that, with Twigs being stubborn and the 3000 finally threatening to send him to the principal's office if he didn't drop it. That of course was an idle threat, for Theodore Wirth Park didn't have a single principal's office in it that I knew of.

"What's a principal's office?" Twigs asked.

Once the 3000 filled him in on that, the big galumpus quickly forgot the matter. That freed the 3000 to translate what Ruth and Birdy were gabbing about.

"He wants to know what she's doing out in a storm like this," the 3000 said. "She told him she's trying to get Twigs home."

Ruth pointed our way. As soon as Birdy checked out

what she was pointing at, he fumbled his Yoda mask, nearly dropping it. That's how bad we startled him.

"Not going," Twigs reminded us.

Wiping the snow off his eyeglasses, Birdy checked us out again. A warm grin lit up his face. I'd seen people light up that way a few times before, like when they spotted an owl sleeping in a tree, or a fawn following her mother, or a turtle trying to climb a curb. At those moments they looked as if they'd just discovered that the world still had some wonder left in it after all. After a bit, Birdy started chattering real excited-like.

"He's asking if Twigs is a woolly mammoth," the 3000 said.

When Ruth answered, Birdy's grin brightened even further and he started hopping up and down. The way his bathrobe flounced was a sight to see. Underneath it were green pants and knee-high red boots. Even the mayor's jaw went slack, and he generally prided himself on having seen everything under the sun, the moon, and anything else passing by overhead.

"He's asking if a spaceship brought you," the 3000 said.

"A what?" Twigs asked.

The 3000 clicked a moment before saying, "It's like a big bird that can fly between planets."

Twigs shuddered. "What's planets?"

"Islands in the sky."

"I never knew—"

"Class, please save your questions," the 3000 said. "I need to follow what these two humans are saying to each other. It may be important."

Just then Ruth was talking. Whatever she said made Birdy yip, cover his mouth in surprise, and pump a fist in celebration. *Yes!* He seemed to be saying.

"Now, what'd she tell him?" the mayor groaned.

"Just that Twigs got here through a rip in the space-time continuum. He's a little disappointed that a spaceship didn't transport him, but apparently has been yearning to see a rip in the space-time continuum, too. He wants to know how big the opening is and if Twigs came alone. And now she's telling him about me."

The 3000 stepped away from Twigs to wave in Birdy's direction. The man lifted his face—his real face—to the falling snow and spread his arms out wide as if his prayers had finally, at long last, been answered. He lit up as if things were only getting better and better.

"Ruth's telling him that I'm an educational robot from the future," the 3000 relayed.

"How's he taking that?" I asked, though really, I could tell without being told. Birdy was beaming as if he could smell freshly baked bread. I had to sneak a sniff to make sure he wasn't.

"Remarkably well," the 3000 said. "Apparently he's been hoping to meet someone from the future for as long as he's been waiting to run into a rip in the space-time continuum."

"Lucky him," the mayor groused. "What else is he going on about?"

"He's wondering if you and Gilly are robots from the future too."

"What gave him that idea?" I asked.

"The way you're talking to each other."

"Now, isn't that just typical?" the mayor groused. "I suppose he thinks animals can't speak to each other. You'd better straighten him out on that."

"I shall," the 3000 promised, and turning to the man, she did.

Slapping his forehead as if he'd been a dunce, Birdy gushed what sounded like an apology and gave us an embarrassed finger-waggle wave.

"He begs your pardon," the robot translated.

"Now what's he doing?" I asked.

"You'll have to tell me," said the 3000, still unable to see.

"He's raised an arm above his head."

"And is jumping up and down," the mayor added with distaste.

The 3000 whirred and clicked a moment before saying, "Perhaps he's raised his hand to ask a question. One moment, please." She and Birdy spoke briefly before she translated again. "He's wondering if he can touch Twigs."

"What's he want to do that for?" the mayor asked, jealous about being overlooked.

"To prove to himself this is really happening."

"What about time contamination?" The mayor could be a real stickler when feeling left out.

"Given our current predicament," the 3000 said, "perhaps it would be permissible. We appear to be in need of this man's goodwill. Twigs, is it all right with you?"

"I guess so." Twigs turned bashful.

The 3000 relayed that to Birdy, who carefully stepped forward, tugged off one of his green-clawed gloves, and gently patted Twigs's trunk while cooing something friendly.

"He's welcoming you to the twenty-first century," the 3000 said, "and is saying he's incredibly honored to meet such a magnificent creature as yourself."

"Oh, please," muttered the mayor.

"A-gosh," Twigs said. "Now would you ask if I could stay with him?"

"Twigs," the 3000 reasoned, "we've been over why you can't—"

A wolf howl interrupted the rest of what the 3000 had to say. A wolf howl that didn't seem too far away.

"The man's saying that he's never heard a wolf in the park," the 3000 reported. "And the girl's telling him that he still hasn't. That it's a caveman who's after Twigs."

Birdy frowned, pointed at something behind us, and shouted.

"Now what?" the mayor asked, refusing to check over his shoulder.

I looked though. The three cavemen had stepped out of the storm, looking different. They'd claimed souvenirs from the house they'd broken into.

Boar-head was wearing a lampshade like a hat. It had small red balls dangling from its bottom that matched up nicely with the red paint on his face.

Wolf-head was holding a mop in place of the spear that the 3000 had ripped away from him. He shook its floppy head at us with confidence.

Leading the way was Saber-tooth. He had draped a pink blanket over his head and shoulders to help stay warm after being dunked in the pond. His teeth were chattering and he was trembling like the last oak leaf clinging to a tree in late fall. But that didn't mean the other two cavemen cut him any slack. They poked his back to keep him moving forward.

Chapter 21

Fzzzzt!

Birdy took charge, shouting orders while tugging on his green claws and head.

"Class," the 3000 announced as if starting a lesson, "this man says he's been waiting all his life for a chance to do something heroic that could save the world."

"Is that what he's up to?" the mayor sounded off.

The 3000 ignored that to say, "He's offering to hold back the caveman while we get away. He suggests we retreat to his garage, where we can hole up until we figure out a way to get Twigs home."

"Not necessary," Twigs insisted.

"Very necessary," the 3000 countered. "And to get to his garage all we have to do is follow the path he's made with his snowblower."

Flinging open his bathrobe, Birdy challenged the cavemen with a shout. At the same time, he whipped out a sword that hung from a belt. The 3000 couldn't translate exactly what he saying, not with the green mask once again muffling the words, but his tone sounded like, *Halt! Take another step closer and I shall banish you to a kingdom beyond the sun.* Or something of that sort. He seemed to be having the time of his life.

I wish I could say that Birdy's sword glinted in the snowblower's headlight, striking fear into the cavemen's hearts. If it had, he might have had a fighting chance. But I'm afraid the sword looked gray and cheap and made of plastic, as if it'd bend or break apart as soon as it struck something solid. Besides, I kind of doubted the cavemen even knew what he was brandishing at them.

They looked more confused than afraid. Birdy's green mask slowed them down more than anything.

But then Birdy turned the sword's handle.

The blade flashed a brilliant green just like the 3000's Newtonian force beam. It also made a *fzzzzt* that sounded electrical.

The cavemen stopped in their tracks.

But even being reminded of the 3000's force beam didn't slow them down for long. A moment later they started moving forward again. Something that Saber-tooth had said angered the two older cavemen into shoving him ahead. The boy's tone said that nobody had mentioned anything about bright green swords when they'd started out after tusks. He might have even gone so far as to suggest they call it day and head home. The two older cavemen weren't having any of that.

I can't be sure, but I think the lampshade and mop and pink blanket scared Twigs more than the clubs and spears had. With a groan, he shuffled through the drifts around the snowblower, heading to the path that Birdy had already cleared. And here's the thing: For a couple

of steps there he didn't hobble, and when he did remember to limp, it was his right front leg that was bothering him. Earlier it'd been his left. This didn't seem like the best time to go into all that, though, so I saved it, thinking I might find a chance to bring it up with the big galumpus when the mayor wasn't sitting beside me. I had a hunch that finding out that Twigs was faking it might set Crawdaddy off.

The last I saw of Birdy?

He'd taken a mighty two-handed swipe with his sword, missing the cavemen altogether. Losing his balance, he'd slipped and fallen to one knee.

Saber-tooth reluctantly shrugged the pink blanket off his shoulders and cast it at Birdy as if it was a magical spell. I never saw what happened next. They all vanished into the snow behind us and Birdy's shouts sounded as if coming from beneath a blanket.

Chapter 22

Alas

The snowblower's path cut straight down the middle of the street but was filling fast. Still, we would have made good time if Twigs hadn't gone back to favoring his leg. Whenever one of the cavemen let loose a whoop, the big galumpus entirely forgot he was lame and speeded up for a few steps. But as soon as the cry faded, he went back to creeping along, with lots of stops and whimpers. Whenever we hit an icy patch beneath the snow? Baby steps.

"Not going back," Twigs vowed along the way.

"Would you rather get poked by that bunch chasing us?" the mayor asked.

His question turned the big galumpus all sullen and nudged him forward, until he remembered a different reason he didn't want to go home.

"There's no room for me back there," he said, without convincing anyone. It sounded like an excuse, and the mayor only had time for those when he was the one making them.

"Even less room here," the mayor answered.

"Looks plenty big to me."

"Only because all this snow hides how cramped everything is," I said, hoping Twigs would understand that we weren't all against him.

We slogged on another few feet.

"Twigs," the 3000 coaxed. "You need to go faster, dear. I fear that the time tunnel won't stay open a lot longer."

"If you're using that leg as an excuse to slow us down," the mayor jumped in, "so help me—"

"I'm trying," Twigs complained, limping a little faster. "I'm trying."

But soon enough he slowed again, whimpering that the pain was too much and that he needed to rest his leg.

While all that was going on, we occasionally heard Birdy behind us, sounding vexed and overmatched and just generally out of sorts. Things couldn't have been going as heroically as he'd hoped.

"Twigs," the 3000 urged, "I'm afraid they're catching up to us."

"Blast them with that green beam of yours," the mayor ordered. "That sent them packing the last time."

"Alas, my force beam remains offline."

"'Alas'?" the mayor griped. That was just the kind of high-sounding word he liked to sprinkle about to impress, and here some green bear from the future with low batteries had beaten him to it. That didn't sit well on top of all our other problems.

Ruth stepped up, offering to hang back and scare off the cavemen with the flash from her camera phone. As soon as the 3000 translated her offer, the mayor was all for it, but the 3000 pointed out that these cavemen weren't any dummies. They'd already been scared off by the camera flash once, so the chances of it working again were extremely low. What the 3000 did suggest was that Ruth run ahead to see how far it was to the garage. She took off at once, leaving the mayor seething because he hadn't been the one to send her. I knew all the signs—stiff back, gums pulled tight, eyeteeth showing. Being bossed around by the 3000 rubbed the mayor wrong, and nothing good ever came from his being rubbed that way.

"I suppose I could play dead again," I offered, feeling plenty droopy about it but also feeling obliged to smooth things over. "That ought to buy the rest of you some time."

"Good thinking, Gilly," the mayor said, looking daggers at the 3000.

Maybe that green bear would have picked up on the trouble that was brewing if she'd been able to see. To make matters stickier, she went out of her way to compliment me.

"Class," the 3000 brightly said, "I hope you have all noticed what Gilly is doing. He is willing to sacrifice himself to save the rest of us, which is the very noblest kind of impulse, but I'm afraid that these cavemen have already seen him play dead. It is unlikely that he'd fool them again. No, at this point, I calculate that our best option is to hole up in the garage. That should give Twigs time to rest his leg while we make him a splint."

"Oh, you've calculated that, have you?" mocked the mayor.

"What's a splint?" Twigs asked.

"Something to help your leg feel better."

"I don't know about that," Twigs stalled once the 3000 filled him in on how splints work.

The big galumpus wasn't the only one unhappy, either. The mayor was acting more put-upon by the second.

"And what about that time tunnel?" the mayor asked. "I thought it wasn't going to stick around forever?"

"It's not," the 3000 agreed. "But if those cavemen catch us out in the open, I fear it won't matter how long the time tunnel stays open."

"Alas," the mayor chimed in, sarcastic-like.

Watching the two of them go at it didn't exactly fill

me or Twigs with hope, but just then Ruth returned, breathless but with good news.

"She says we're almost to the garage," said the 3000.

Hearing that, we forged ahead, but even though we were moving faster, it did seem to take the longest time to get there.

And all the while the mayor was harboring the last thing you ever wanted a raccoon to harbor—a grudge.

And the 3000 was flickering like a streetlight about to call it quits.

And Twigs did his best to remember to limp while wishing he was somewhere else. "Take me away, take me away, take me away," he chanted under his breath. But his wisher remained broken.

And Ruth gave the galumpus an endless pep talk, or at least that's what it sounded like to me, all heartfelt and upbeat.

The whole world was snow and nothing but snow, and yet it didn't feel as if there was enough of it to ever hide us from all the eyes watching our retreat. On top of which, a perfect slash of lightning laid out the street as bright as broad daylight. The rumble that followed it made me wonder if a huge chunk of the park hadn't fallen off.

And just in case all that wasn't enough, Birdy's distant shouts died completely away. But the whoops from the cavemen? They only grew stronger.

Hearing them speeded Twigs up for several steps until he remembered that going faster moved him closer to where he kept saying he didn't want to go—home. Then his leg went stiff all over again. He dragged it along as if it belonged to someone else. Putting weight on it made him grunt and straighten out his trunk and whimper things like, "I can't keep going."

"Oh yes you can," said the mayor.

Finally, the path before us curved up a driveway and straight into a garage with a wide-open door. A light was burning inside the garage. I'd never noticed before how welcoming a light could be. I usually steered away from the things, unless hunting moths, but this once I was grateful to be headed toward one. It showed there wasn't anyone lurking inside the garage, waiting to pulverize the next galumpus headed that way.

Glancing behind us, Ruth shouted something considerably overheated. That's when I saw the cavemen charging up the cleared driveway. They weren't blowing kisses, either. They were waving their club and spear and mop, and sounding as though screaming the awfullest kinds of threats and mean-hearted promises. The light in the garage didn't slow them down a bit. Breaking into houses had taught them that lights didn't bite. To speed us along, the 3000 translated some of what they were screaming.

"We got you now!"

"Supper's served!"

"Did you miss us?"

We screeched and wailed and bumbled ahead in one breath-sucking panic, sounding doomed as the morning star. Ruth was down to one word of encouragement, which she wailed over and over. I'm guessing it was *Run! Run!*

In all the excitement, the 3000 went silent. Her green glow quit flickering and slowly slid away like a leaf sinking to the bottom of a pond. Watching her go dark was awful, just awful, and all our hopes went dark with her. Her dimming tickled the cavemen no end. They gamboled about, rubbing their tummies as if they would soon be going to be full of warm, good things that used to be us. A double crash of lightning only made them merrier. For a minute or two Saber-tooth actually forgot that his robe was frozen solid and he'd lost his pink blanket and that Boar-head and Wolf-head still expected him to finish what he'd started.

Never having met up with a garage, the cavemen had no idea that we could close its door in their faces. They thought they could follow us right inside and do all the nasty, terrible, I'd-rather-not-say kind of things they'd been promising. Assuming they had us cornered, they took their time, taunting us and congratulating themselves, and making sure Saber-tooth led the way so that he could prove himself all grown up.

When they finally did get around to pouncing, they had to go after the 3000 first. The green bear still had enough power left to hold on to Twigs's tail, which made her the last one into the garage.

Same as before, Saber-tooth's spear glanced off the 3000's metal-and-plastic hide without knocking her over. Now her green fur blinked out all at once! But not before she managed to kick backward with just enough strength to knock Saber-tooth into Wolf-head. They both went sprawling down the snowy driveway. Boar-head had to dodge them, giving Ruth time to punch a button on the wall. The garage door came *rackety-rack-rack*ing down, making such a startling noise that everyone screamed and jumped in fright all over again.

"Somewhere else!" Twigs cried out, straining to wish himself away.

Seeing the garage door lowering right in front of them made those cavemen's faces longer by half. Cliff swallows could have flown in and out of their mouths, wide open as they'd flopped. The last I saw of them before the door closed? They were all scrambling and grabbing ahold of each other and sliding backward as if the garage was something alive that was swallowing us and coming after them next. Saber-tooth even slipped us a goodbye wave, with a sheepish little grin, as if he wasn't all that sorry to see us go. Maybe now he wouldn't have to prove himself to his pa.

Then we had the garage to ourselves.

Chapter 23

Inverse Time-Ratio Paradox

A wonderful feeling of relief flooded me, though not for long. A crash put an end to it. Looking behind Twigs, I saw that the 3000 had fallen flat on her face. She lay still as a tree but nowhere near as green. She remained completely dark. Same as a fallen tree, she wasn't making the slightest sound. Not a *click* or *whir* or *tiddly-tum*.

It felt as crowded as a raspberry patch in that garage, and about as prickly. Such close quarters made steam rise off us. The woolly mammoth's earthiness blossomed considerably, leaving me awfully puckered up around my nose. To one side a pickup truck crowded us. On the other side a workbench stretched out, with tools hanging on the wall behind it. I saw hammers and saws and a bunch of other gizmos that I didn't really have time to wonder about, not with the way we were all trying to talk at once.

"What happened?" cried Twigs.

"Perfect timing," said the mayor, acting as if he'd always known that the 3000 would conk out right when we needed her most.

"Is she sleeping?" I asked, grasping at straws.

The mayor laughed as if surrounded by simpletons when he heard that one. I had half a mind to tell him off, and I probably would have if we hadn't had bigger problems, what with the 3000 stretched out cold on the garage floor.

Ruth was talking too. She'd kneeled beside the 3000, shaking the bear's shoulder and telling her to get up, or at least I guessed that's what she was saying as she pressed an ear against the 3000's back. What she

212

expected to hear going on inside there, I can't say, but after a bit, she gave up listening and shook her head slow and weary-like, letting us know it was hopeless. Pinch-faced and grave as she looked, I had an idea that something was about to break down inside her, too.

"Try flipping her over," I urged, wanting to be helpful.

Okay, okay, I'd forgotten that Ruth couldn't understand a word I was saying. That was a low point.

"See what you've gotten us into?" the mayor complained.

Hearing that was another low.

"Gilly?" Ruth said, along with a string of other words that were as meaningless to me as mine were to her. More lowness.

And there were even lower points headed our way. We reached one about two seconds later.

"We're probably better off without her," Twigs sniffled. The way his voice cracked? He knew that wasn't true even as he said it.

"Nice try," the mayor spitefully complimented, "but you're still going home."

That kicked off a squabble that peppered the air and was about as grown up as a week-old possum clinging to his mother's pouch. Another low point.

Not to be outdone, the cavemen regrouped outside the garage and did some shouting of their own. When it came to name-calling, they didn't sound like any slouches, either, though their taunts remained untranslated.

I screamed for quiet, without luck, but Ruth came up with a way to shut up Twigs and the mayor. Pulling off her mittens, she ran her hands all over the 3000's shoulders and back, legs and feet, as if searching for something beneath the bear's park ranger uniform. A button or switch, maybe. I'd noticed that humans were awfully big on turning things off and on, and at the moment it beat any other ideas being passed around. The mayor and Twigs actually quit going after each other to see what Ruth might find.

Eventually, Ruth tried flipping the 3000 over to examine the robot's front, but she wasn't strong enough to do it.

"Twigs," I said, "help."

"Why should I?"

Fortunately I didn't have to answer that. The cavemen answered it for me by slapping their hands against the garage door and shaking it as if trying to tear it loose. Hearing that convinced the big galumpus to wrap his trunk around the 3000 and roll her over.

Ruth continued her examination of the 3000, giving the bear's ears and nose an especially close look. She peered into them with the help of the light on her phone, but in the end, all she could do was shrug and shake her head as if all was lost and not about to be found.

I have no idea what would have happened next if the storm hadn't come to our rescue. But it did. A crack of lightning and roll of thunder nearly shook the garage apart.

A split-second later, a boom sounded outside. That lightning bolt must have missed us by a whisker. Close by, a crash rang out that tingled my bottom. I never did get a chance to wonder how that worked. I mean, wasn't it more likely that some other part of me—my ears or nose or something—would have tingled before my bottom? But less than a heartbeat later the light in the garage went out, leaving everything dark but the light on Ruth's phone.

"What's going on?" quaked Twigs.

"Perfect," cursed the mayor.

"Everyone stay calm," I advised, hoping to settle Twigs down.

I'm not sure how long the ceiling light stayed out. Long enough for the cavemen to start yapping again outside the garage, no doubt threatening the most amazing kinds of hair-raising things.

Ruth shined her phone light around, making everyone's eyes glow until without warning the power returned and the garage's ceiling light blinked back to life. We were all standing exactly where we'd been when it had gone off, except that Ruth was gazing up at the bulb as if she'd never seen one before. Something told me she was having herself some kind of inspiration about what powered the bulb and whether it could also help bring the 3000 around. That was good. We were in bad need of a brilliant idea.

Rising, she rummaged about the garage until finding a long orange cord. I'd seen similar cords attached to strings of twinkling colored lights in people's yards. She plugged one end of the cord into a small box on the wall and jammed the other end into the 3000's mouth as if feeding her.

Seconds later the 3000's eyelids fluttered open. There still wasn't any light in her eyes, but just having them open was enough progress to make it seem as if we weren't sunk yet. A minute later her fur ruffled a bit, regaining a weak, green-some glow that gradually grew stronger. A minute after that, the 3000 sat up, tugged the orange cord out of her mouth, and stuck it in her ear as if that's where it really belonged. She twisted her neck to work out a kink and poked her nose as if pressing a button.

"Class?" the 3000 called out, her eyes still dark. "What has happened?"

"The cavemen have us trapped in this garage," the mayor told her. "Just like I warned they would."

"But at least we're safe," I pointed out.

"For how long?" Mayor Crawdaddy fired back.

Ruth said something while holding up her cell phone.

"Now what's she want?" Crawdaddy asked.

"To call for help," said the 3000. "But I'm afraid the authorities will create more problems than solutions. If news of time-travel educational programs from the future leaks out today, the programs might be banned as too dangerous, which would leave me without a future to return to."

"Oh, pshaw!" interrupted the mayor, tired of listening. His attention span always had been short as a gnat's, unless the topic was him.

"But you see, class," the 3000 went on, "I'm worried that if we don't get everyone back to where they belong before they're discovered by the people of today, well, the inverse time-ratio paradox might come into play."

"Are you trying to make my head spin?" the mayor accused.

"Not at all. I'm simply sharing basic temporal theorems with you. A time traveler to the past can alter the future without even meaning to."

"How's that?" The mayor wasn't buying it.

"By changing an event that alters the course of history. If I go into the past and do something that prevents your grandparents from ever meeting, what do you think would happen to you?"

"Spare me the what-ifs," the mayor warned. "And stay away from my granny."

I stepped in, saying, "I think she's trying to tell us that changing the past could change the world as we know it. And not getting Twigs back to his own time would be changing the past."

"I'm afraid so," the 3000 agreed, sounding rather guilty for a robot.

"And whose fault is that?" the mayor asked.

"Most definitely mine," the 3000 conceded. "That's why I'm doing everything I can to get Twigs back to the time tunnel before it collapses."

I started taking a real liking to that green bear. She may not have been anything but a fancy box of nuts and bolts and fake fur and busted subroutines, but she did stand up and take the blame for her mistakes, which put her one up on certain parties I shall leave unnamed.

"Oh, fiddle faddle," complained the mayor.

At which point a new voice spoke up. Well, maybe it wasn't so much new as belonging to someone we hadn't heard from in a while, someone that I wouldn't have minded not hearing from for a while longer, either. It was an awfully all-knowing and tiresome kind of voice.

"Say, now," the new voice barged in, "maybe this is nowhere near as big a deal as you fools seem to think. Maybe all we have to do is tell those cavemen we'll help them get home. That ought to be worth something."

Yes, the Earl of Sussex had caught up to us.

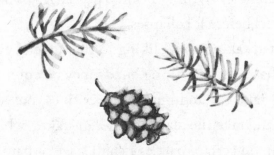

Chapter 24

Mayor Crawdaddy and a Moment of Glory

That garage was getting more crowded by the second. Everybody but me jerked toward the new voice. I just closed my eyes in misery, recognizing Sussex's nonsense on the spot. How he'd caught up to us didn't take long to figure out, either. He came crawling out from beneath Twigs, where he'd been clinging to the big galumpus's furry belly since we'd all gone sliding and screaming down that hill in one big pile. Why hadn't he spoken up until now? Knowing Sussex, he'd been biding his time, waiting for a chance to make a grand entrance. As he climbed up the woolly mammoth's shaggy side, I only had one question: How had he managed to stay quiet for so long? It had to be some kind of record for him.

"You ninny!" the mayor blazed. "What makes you think those cavemen want to go home? All the loot they're grabbing? They might get it in their heads to stay here awhile."

"Handing over the galumpus might change their minds about that," Sussex said, unable to drop his earlier suggestion. He acted as if repeating a bad idea might turn it into a good one.

His remark caught everyone but the mayor off-guard. The raccoon twirled his snowy whiskers as if finally willing to consider what Sussex was saying. The mayor had pulled similar dastardly stunts before, claiming they were for the good of the park, but this one seemed a stretch even for him. No one knew what to say, not even Twigs, who developed a stutter on the spot.

"Y-y-you wouldn't do that, w-w-would you?"

"Class," the 3000 chided, "turning Twigs over to the cavemen doesn't strike me as advisable."

Right away Ruth wanted to know what had Twigs so upset. When the 3000 translated everything, she shouted something that could only have meant *No way!* She acted ready to brain the Earl of Sussex with something considerably heavier than a carrot.

"I don't see why not," Sussex said defensively. "It'd take care of all our problems."

Now, that was wrong in so many different directions that it was embarrassing. But what was even more troubling was how long it took someone to tell him to drop it. I'd like to think we were too flabbergasted to know what to say, but maybe we were just as scared as Sussex was and searching for our own way out. Eventually I couldn't take it anymore, not with Twigs twisting his head this way and that to see why we'd turned so quiet on his shoulders. His eyes were wild. Deep down in his throat a whimper was shimmying about.

"Hold on," I told Sussex. "You know what they'd do to him, don't you?"

"Now, how would I know that?" he answered, all offended-like, as if I'd just called his father a chipmunk. "Maybe they're here to take him home. Did you ever think of that?"

"Ain't going home!" Twigs cried out.

Wasn't it about time for Mayor Crawdaddy to step up and do some mayoring? A first-rate plan to get us out of this mess would have been well received. Even a so-so plan wouldn't have been turned down. At the very least he could have reminded us that we were supposed to be making Twigs a splint so that he could move faster. When he didn't jump right in, I raised my eyebrows to let him know that we were all waiting for him to take charge. He didn't appreciate that, as I soon found out.

"Sussex," the mayor griped, "you're pitiful as a dust bath. We're not going to hand this youngster over to a bunch of hungry cavemen, not so long as I'm still the mayor of this park, we're not. We've got rules around here. And even if we didn't, you know and I know that they're not here to take him home, at least not in one piece, they're not. Shame on you for pretending otherwise."

Now and then the mayor had himself a moment of glory that left me proud to be his assistant and maybe just a little ashamed for thinking small of him. Hearing the 3000 translate what he'd said sure earned him Ruth's full backing. Sussex, not so much.

"All right," the Earl came back, "how are *you* going to get those cavemen to leave us alone?"

"Well," the mayor answered, doing his best to sound sincere—and allow me to say, with as much electioneering as he'd done over the years, his best was as smooth and well worn as a stone on a beach—"I was getting to that."

A bubbly, gassy feeling started rising in me, same as it did whenever the mayor promised to get something done.

"So, Gilly," the mayor pushed on, about to even the score for my cocking an eyebrow at him, "know anyone who could lend us a hand?"

I wasn't about to fess up that I couldn't think of a single soul, not with the mayor acting so smug, I wasn't. We might have been trapped in a garage that was surrounded by cavemen armed with clubs and spears and mops. And we might—or might not—have had an injured galumpus on our hands who didn't want to go home, and dash it all, we might have also had a banged-up Smokey 3000 who we didn't know how to help. All this might have been happening in the middle of the worst blizzard in Theodore Wirth's entire history, but I wasn't anywhere near ready to give the mayor the satisfaction of hearing me say I was drawing a blank, even if *blank* barely begins to describe how empty my head felt right about then. What saved me was Twigs, who bought some time by speaking up.

"I can tell you one thing," the woolly mammoth said, eager to get off the subject of handing him over to the cavemen. "This ain't the cave I came through. It's not big enough."

That gave my tail a twist. Hearing Twigs mistake a garage for a cave brought on a sudden insight of my own. Maybe he'd mistaken something over by the creek for a cave. A lot of things can change in ten thousand years. Heck and bottle tops—look how much had changed since just last week, when there hadn't been a scrap of snow cover anywhere in the park. We might find that time tunnel yet, if only we could pull together and get past the welcoming committee waiting outside the garage.

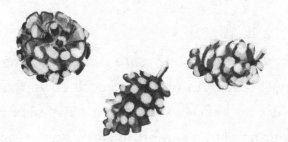

Chapter 25

Furry Boots, Knobby Knees

A **bam-bam-bam cut short my** noodling. Boar-head must have been trying to knock down the garage door with his club. Coming from ten thousand years ago, figuring out how to lift the door was beyond him, and the garage didn't have any windows they could smash and crawl through.

Then came a jingling that must have been Wolf-head shaking his mop at us as if its secret powers would open the door. He was chanting something, too.

Even Saber-tooth got into the act, jabbing his spear under the door in a half-hearted kind of way, as if too wet and cold to care.

It sounded as though they were all done being afraid of the garage. They made promises that the 3000 translated and I'd rather not repeat. In general, they told us the end was coming, and coming fast. They even threatened to start a fire and smoke us out.

Talking about fire made Twigs blurt, "That's bad! We got to get out of here!"

"I'm with the galumpus on this one," the mayor said, twitching his nose as if he'd caught a whiff of something smoky.

Me, I didn't even go there. Next I'd be hearing wind chimes.

"What about your banged-up leg?" Sussex asked the galumpus.

"It's feeling better," Twigs promised.

"Oh yeah?" the mayor said, turning suspicious. "How'd that happen so fast?"

"I don't know," Twigs answered, panicking. "It just did. We got to go!"

So much for bothering with a splint.

By then Twigs's trunk was waving all over the place, and he was short of breath, and he was hopping from foot to foot as if the garage floor was getting hot, which it wasn't. Or at least none of the snow that had fallen off us was melting on it. And there was one last thing that was strange. Twigs had dropped the wishing-he-was-somewhere-else stuff and replaced it with a whimper that went, "I'm sorry . . . I'm sorry . . . I'm sorry . . ."

I had no idea why he'd given up on the wishing and even less idea what he was feeling so sorry about, and there really wasn't time to ask. Right about then I caught a whiff of something burning. A tendril of smoke came curling under the garage door. Either I was about to find myself on my mother's back and headed for a vision, or those cavemen weren't fooling around. They'd managed to start a fire in the middle of a blizzard. That little turtle shell hanging off Wolf-head's belt must have had some awfully useful gear in it. I hadn't given these guys anywhere near enough credit.

All of that together got me wondering if there

mightn't be another path out of that garage, one that led away from cavemen and smoke. I was thinking of a back door. Finding one of those ought to at least shut up the mayor, and maybe save us to boot.

And lo and behold, when I looked, I found one, though there was one teensy-weensy problem with it. The pickup partially blocked the way there. And even if we could have squeezed past the truck, I had serious doubts that Twigs would have been able to fit through the door. The thing was too narrow.

That got me to thinking about the truck, though. The Smokey 3000 couldn't see to drive, but what if . . .

"Smokey," I said, "would you ask Ruth if she knows how to drive a truck?"

"What good's that going to do us?" Sussex scoffed.

"Maybe she can drive us out of here."

"What about Twigs?" the mayor asked, turning all high and mighty, as if he'd caught me turning my back on the galumpus.

"He'd come with us," I said, coughing in the rising smoke. "In back."

"And how are you going to get him up there?"

He had me there, but the 3000 stepped in before I had to admit it.

"I should be able to lift him up there."

That green bear must have had some muscles.

"Are you sure?" I asked.

"It will drain my battery again," the 3000 answered. "But I calculate I can manage it."

So the 3000 asked Ruth if she knew how to drive the pickup, but she only laughed in disbelief.

"She says no," relayed the 3000. "She's barely twelve and no one's ever taught her how to drive."

Just then Wolf-head shouted something that sounded like an ultimatum, particularly when the 3000 translated it as, "Last chance!"

Giving up on the pickup, I started checking out all the tools hanging above the workbench. The mayor and Sussex kept everyone entertained by chattering back at the cavemen, who returned the favor, slapping the garage door for emphasis. Mostly I had no idea what all the tools were used for, until I saw a leaf blower. It wasn't likely I'd ever forget one of those. Last fall Ruth's dad had rousted me from beneath their hot tub with one of them.

"Are you nuts?" the Earl of Sussex cried when I pointed out the leaf blower and suggested using it.

Nobody had a better plan, though. As a matter of fact, nobody else had any kind of plan at all, unless you counted trying to talk the cavemen to death. The way the mayor and Sussex were running their mouths, they acted as if willing to give it a try, but the Smokey 3000 backed me, saying that a good dose of modern technology might be just the thing.

"Class," the 3000 said, "think of this leaf blower as a primitive version of my Newtonian force beam, which the cavemen have already encountered and wished they hadn't. One blast from it may convince them to run."

That won over the mayor and Sussex, that and the way the smoke was filling the garage.

Somehow we got Twigs turned around so that he was facing the door. It took some maneuvering, cramped as it was in there, but at least Twigs's hurt leg stayed better. We unplugged the 3000 from the orange cord stuck in her ear and connected it to the leaf blower instead.

Gripping the leaf blower with both hands, Ruth stepped in front of the Twigs and gave us a countdown, or at least that's what the 3000 claimed she was doing.

"Three, two, one . . ."

I never heard the 3000 say *one*. Ruth fired up the leaf blower and hit the button for the garage door first.

The roar of the leaf blower totally spooked Twigs. He shied away from it as if about to be gobbled up, nearly trampling the 3000, who was holding on to his tail. The Earl of Sussex couldn't take the noise either and was rooting around, trying to crawl beneath me. The mayor

was shouting in my ear, though I couldn't hear what. All three of us were crouched low as we could get on Twigs's back, tight as stick burrs.

As for the 3000, her head was spinning around as if trying to locate where the roar was coming from. Small and crowded as that garage was, the sound thundered down on us from everywhere at once.

Worst of all, as the garage door went up, we found the cavemen standing right outside, ready to lower the kaboom on us. First we saw their furry boots, followed by their knobby knees and animal-skin robes. And right

in front of them crackled a small garbage fire that out-smelled the inside of an old tennis shoe, maybe because a red tennie sat atop the crackling flames. Saber-tooth had crowded close to it, trying to stop his teeth from chattering.

The leaf blower blasted the cavemen like a cyclone, knocking their tangled hair straight back. Their matted beards got parted. The way their eyes looked peeled and their mouths so round? They must have been screaming for mercy. Not that we could hear them above the roar of the leaf blower.

As for the cavemen's fire, the leaf blower knocked it to bits.

Old Wolf-head was the first to turn tail and run. He didn't waste any time checking to see if the other two were following him, either.

Boar-head started backpedaling for all he was worth and wildly swinging his club and shouting threats, I guess. You could see his mouth moving but couldn't catch a word of what he was saying, not with the blower going.

And then there was Saber-tooth. He stood planted

in place with a strange, thrilled grin scrunching up his face even if he was freezing. I almost got the idea he was secretly cheering us on. Ruth got close enough to jab him in the gut with the leaf blower's nozzle before he jumped straight backward. Landing, he spun around and tore off into the blizzard, laughing his head off as if the whole world had gone crazy.

Ruth gave chase, making it halfway down the drive before the orange cord reached its end and the blower came unplugged, dying with a wheeze.

Ruth yelled at us, dropping the blower and waving us ahead.

"She's telling us to follow her," the 3000 said.

She didn't need to ask twice. Now that Twigs had quit pretending to be lame, we cleared out of there fast, bowling over one of Birdy's neighbors who'd stepped outside to check out the ruckus. His dumbfounded expression as we charged past left me wondering if I looked as lost and confused as he did.

Chapter 26

Jingle Bells

A half-block later, Twigs was back to limping, on his right front leg this time. We came to a stop.

"Now what?" the mayor snapped. "You were fine just a minute ago."

"It hurts again," Twigs whimpered.

"Say," Sussex jumped in, "wasn't it your other leg that was bothering you?"

"What other one?" Twigs asked, acting as if he had so many legs hurting him that he couldn't keep track.

"Twigs," I coaxed, "is there something you're not telling us?"

"Not really."

He might have convinced a freshly hatched gosling with a fib that wishy-washy, but not a thoroughbred liar like the mayor.

"Come on," Crawdaddy ordered. "Out with it."

"You're with friends," I reminded him.

"I'm thinking it was the other foot," Sussex insisted.

"Class," the 3000 refereed, "one speaker at a time, please."

I suppose we might have gone around and around like that till the blizzard petered out, and knowing how the mayor and Sussex liked to listen to themselves, maybe we would have, if the cavemen hadn't got to whooping it up behind us again. They weren't too far back, either. One peep from them was all it took to start Twigs off again, this time favoring his left foot.

To reach the creek we only had to follow the street in front of Birdy's house. The mayor, Sussex, and I managed to agree on that much. Whether we'd find a cave by the creek, whether the 3000 would make it that far, whether Twigs was limping on the same foot as before—all that was up for grabs.

Naturally the mayor put himself in charge of steering. Feeling overlooked, Sussex served up enough free advice to spin a whirligig. I sat with them on Twigs's shoulder hump, keeping a darty eye on everything behind us. The 3000 traipsed along, clinging to Twigs's tail and every once in a while giving off a *whir-click-ping* that made her flicker. Ruth? She brought up the rear, walking backward to watch for cavemen. The falling snow kept right on keeping us company.

But in the end what we had to worry about wasn't behind us at all. It was up ahead. People were singing up there.

"What's that?" the mayor asked after shushing Sussex.

At first I couldn't tell what I was hearing either. It almost sounded like a twitter bush. Sometimes sparrows will flock to a bush and chirp up a storm at the unlikeliest of times, like, say, in a blizzard, to keep their spirits up. But it didn't quite sound like that, either.

Maybe something was humming in one of the houses we were passing.

But bit by bit, as the noise became clearer, I could tell it wasn't birds in a bush or pipes in a house. It was people. Singing people. They were belting out a rousing tune, which gave me something new to wonder about. What had put them in a rollicking good mood? The storm? Or something else? When it came to people, it was often best not to know the answer to questions like that. Such answers could raise all kinds of complications, like the time I strayed too close to picnickers singing around a cake lit with candles. It had turned out they weren't willing to share a slice.

And one last thing: There was a dog with the people singing in front of us. A barking, yapping, baying dog who sounded on the trail of something juicy, like, say, a possum.

It was the barking that halted us.

"What's that?" Twigs asked, confused.

"Trouble," the mayor grimly answered.

He'd had a couple of run-ins with dogs over the years and would tell you all about them if you're weren't careful. For that matter, most anyone who lived in the park knew about dogs. You didn't last long if you didn't.

"So what's the plan?" Sussex pestered in a satisfied kind of way, as if he reckoned the mayor was in over his head.

"We could try feeding you to them," the mayor suggested, sounding more out of sorts by the second. "Gilly, why don't you slip on ahead and scout around a bit, see what we're up against."

"Wouldn't it be easier to steer away from them on a side street?" I asked.

"In a storm like this?" the mayor said, astounded. "We'd only end up lost."

I couldn't argue with that. The snow was coming down worse than ever. The farther we went, the poorer the visibility. At least we knew that the street we were on eventually led to the creek.

"Wouldn't Sussex be a better choice?" I suggested. "What with all his talents?"

"He has a point," Sussex couldn't help but agree.

"Balderdash!" the mayor spat out. "The little runt would get lost in the first snowdrift, and even if he didn't, he'd probably run off and leave us at the mercy of whatever's headed our way."

"Is he that bad?" Twigs wanted to know.

"Worse," the mayor promised.

"Oh yeah," Sussex boasted, relishing the spotlight.

"He's probably already dreaming up some story about how we got torn to shreds by a pack of snow-crazed dogs," the mayor went on, "and how he did everything in his powers to save us, but there were too many of them, and in the end he didn't have any choice but to abandon us so that someone would live to tell the tale."

"A-gosh."

Trust me, none of that left me feeling any braver. Screwing up my courage, I said, "What about you, Mayor? Your eyes are way better than mine."

Which was true, if we were looking for excuses.

"Gilligan," the mayor sternly lectured, "you know darn well that somebody's got to stay here with this galumpus. If you don't come back, it will fall to me to save the park by getting him home."

"Ain't going," Twigs felt obliged to say.

"But what if I get up there and have, you know, one of my bouts?" I asked, dancing around my reputation for keeling over dead at the worst possible time.

"Don't," the mayor advised.

"But what if I do?" I persisted. "It's not exactly something I can always control, you know, and if I do run into trouble, well, then, sometimes, well, you know what happens."

"What happens?" Twigs whispered.

"He plays dead," Sussex chirped, enjoying himself no end.

"He does?" Twigs gasped.

"It's been known to happen," I admitted. "And if it does happen, I wouldn't be able to come back and tell you what I'd seen, so maybe I'm not the best—"

"Gilly," the mayor interrupted, "we've got complete confidence in you."

Now, that was pure moonbeams. He didn't mean a word of it and was only trying to save his own neck.

"Shake a leg," Sussex added.

"Go see what you can see," the mayor ordered. "And if you get a chance, lead them off down a side street so that we can stay on this one."

All that give and take meant the voices kept getting closer. By then they were near enough to tell that one of them was a terrible singer, and some of them were giggling. I couldn't be sure, but it sounded as if there were at least twenty or thirty of them, no doubt marauding through the storm for the frightfulest kinds of reasons. How did I know that? Common sense. There hadn't been anything good happen to us yet, had there? So why would our luck change now?

And I decided it wasn't just one dog I was hearing. Couldn't be. There was too much growling and snarling mixed in with the barking for it to be coming from only one dog. No, it sounded like there was an entire pack of slobbering, hungry, Northwoods dogs named Slasher or Fang or Old Rip headed our way.

"Go on now." The mayor nudged me toward the edge of Twigs's back. "You're always going on about how you think you could do more."

"I am?"

"Don't be shy," Sussex razzed.

"Here's your big chance," the mayor said.

They were doing their level best to back me into a corner. I sort of remembered complaining once, or maybe twice, about how the mayor never put any trust in me. Now it was all coming back to bite me. What with all the barking up ahead, that was an unfortunate a way to think of it. Whenever anyone in the park got to talking about how they wanted to leave this world, being helped on their way by a dog always landed at the bottom of the list.

"Anybody know what they're singing about?" I asked, taking a sudden interest in anything that kept me from leaving.

"Their song is called 'Jingle Bells,'" the 3000 reported. "It's a popular tune of this time period."

"Do you know anything about who might be likely to sing it?" I asked.

"Most anyone," the 3000 said.

"Any idea why they might sing it?" I stalled.

"Gilly, if you don't get your miserable tail moving . . ." the mayor warned.

My procrastinations paid off before he could finish his threat.

A man in a red-checkered cap stepped out of the snow falling in front of us. He didn't see us at first. His head was down as he pulled on a rope that was draped over his shoulder. His singing was as heartfelt as one of Gigi's lullabies; though more rambunctious.

Tied to the other end of the rope he was pulling came a wooden toboggan. You saw them at the park's sledding hill sometimes. Riding on the toboggan was a pair of little kids in puffy snowsuits, one blue, one pink.

At the very back of the toboggan rode a loaf-sized white dog, a real flopsy-mopsy who'd caught our scent and was growling and snapping all ferocious-like. It kind of looked like an act, given how his bushy tail was wagging at the same time. He had so much curly hair that you couldn't see his eyes to tell for sure. Except for his black nose, he thoroughly blended in with the blizzard, especially when he quit barking to give himself a good shake that sent sticky snow flying. At least he wasn't one of those haughty dogs who pretended they couldn't understand animal talk.

"Who's coming?" the dog barked over and over. "Who's coming? State your business. These people are under my protection and I will bite. Who's coming?"

Standard dog talk.

I braced myself, expecting the rest of the pack to come busting out of the storm any second, lunging and chomping, but it never happened. At some point I realized that I might have overestimated the number of snap-happy dogs headed our way. Maybe I'd been a little high on how many marauding singers, too.

As for what the mayor and Sussex were thinking, I didn't have to waste time wondering. They came right out and shared it.

"Now you've done it," said the mayor.

"Thanks a bunch," Sussex quickly heaped on.

They were talking to me, blaming me. It didn't seem right. It didn't seem fair. But whatever happened next was going to be pinned on me for not following the mayor's orders and leading the singers away down a side street. The fact that I didn't tell them off on the spot left me feeling so low and cowardly and down on myself that I nearly slid off Twigs's back to slink out of sight into the nearest snowbank. But leaving Twigs in Sussex and the mayor's care wouldn't have been fair, either, so I stuck it out.

"What's that?" Twigs was pointing his trunk at the dog, who'd stopped barking the instant he'd spotted Twigs.

It turned out I wasn't the only one who suffered bouts of cowardice. That dog was doing his best to hide behind the two kids in the puffy snowsuits.

"A dog," the 3000 explained.

"What's that?"

"A descendant of a wolf."

"You're kidding," Twigs said.

"Not at all," the 3000 assured him. "But don't worry, the fact that he's quit barking most likely means he's friendly."

That robot should have kept that last thought to herself. It would have saved us a whole lot of trouble.

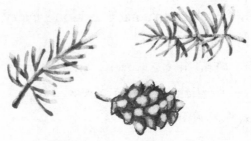

Chapter 27

Sparky Xavier

The man in the red-checkered cap wiped his eyes with a gloved hand as if it would help him understand what he was seeing. I suppose a woolly mammoth with a raccoon, possum, and red squirrel hitching a ride on his back didn't happen along every day, not even in a blizzard.

And if *we* weren't enough to take in, there was a green flickering bear dressed in a park ranger's uniform right behind us.

And wouldn't you know, right then three wolf howls rose from farther behind us. It was probably just the storm distorting things, but it sounded as though they were about to pounce any second.

The man pulled his kids closer to him as their singing cut out. They were all gawking our way, and the kid in pink was tugging on the dad's sleeve, asking him something awfully careful-like. He patted the child's hand without glancing away from us.

The curly-haired dog at the back of the toboggan was watching us closely too. He growled deep in his throat, warning us to keep our distance.

"These people are under my protection," the dog repeated.

Ruth approached them, talking to the father in the friendliest kind of way, but he stayed put and let fly a couple of uneasy questions. His eyes kept shifting from Twigs's tusks, to the three of us on Twigs's back, to the 3000 flickering behind us. He double-checked the 3000 every time. Whenever he asked a question, Ruth answered real earnest. I wouldn't have minded hearing how she was explaining everything, but Twigs got it in his head to strike up a conversation with the dog first.

"You got a nice family there," Twigs said without so much as an introduction, although he took care of that next. "My name's Twigs. I'm from the Dragonfly Creek herd, and am a long, long way from home, which is a whole lot friendlier place than here. Who are you?"

The big galumpus's friendliness caught the little dog off-guard and he answered, "Sparky Xavier, though most call me just Sparky."

That encouraged Twigs to step closer, though right away the father moved his sled back two steps. What the man would have heard was his dog growling and Twigs blatting, so for all he knew they were threatening each other instead of making friends. He wasn't the only one making a mistake about what was going on. I'm afraid we'd all underestimated how badly the galumpus didn't want to go home, though we were about to find out.

"This bunch has kidnapped me," Twigs blurted to the dog before we could stop him. "They're making me go along with them against my will."

"Why, that's not right," said Sparky, stepping off the toboggan.

"Hold on now," the mayor said. "He's making that up."

As usual, raccoons and dogs got along about as well as snapping turtles and anything else.

"Oh yeah?" Sparky came right back. "And just why would he do that?"

"Probably because he figures you're a soft touch," Sussex spouted, diplomatic as ever.

Red squirrels and dogs? More snapping turtles.

I tried to settle everyone down by explaining, "He's a little upset because of the cavemen."

"What cavemen?" Sparky asked, casting about as if I were making things up.

Possums and dogs? Not quite snapping turtles, but close.

"The ones howling like wolves," Sussex told him.

Naturally the cavemen chose then to go silent. The sound of glass breaking in a nearby house probably explained why.

"You three have an answer for everything, don't you?" Sparky said.

The 3000 quit crackling and flickering long enough to ask, "Class, to whom are you talking?"

Up to then the dog hadn't seen the 3000. Twigs had been blocking his view.

"Who's that?" Sparky growled, looking around the big galumpus.

Neither the mayor nor Sussex wanted to tackle that one, so I took a shot at it, saying, "That's a robot from the future. She's trying to help us get this woolly mammoth back to the past, where he belongs."

"Don't you believe them!" Twigs cried.

"'Deed I won't," Sparky promised. "I wasn't born yesterday."

"Thank goodness," Twigs sobbed.

"What's a woolly mammoth?" asked Sparky.

"Search me," Twigs said. "They keep calling me one, but I'm a camel."

"I thought so," Sparky said, sounding an awful lot like he had been born yesterday. "Just where are these bandits trying to take you, anyway?"

"I don't know," Twigs groaned. "Someplace terrible where there's fences."

"The ruffians!"

"Do you suppose," Twigs pleaded, "that I could come live with your family? I'd feel ever so much safer with you."

Of all the ungrateful . . .

"I don't see why not," Sparky said. "Just last week they let this boy here bring home a hamster."

"What's that?"

"A furry little thing that likes to hide out and nibble on seeds and go around sniffing everything. Pretty helpless, but I watch out for him. And the boy got to bring the hamster home because the week before his sister dragged home a goldfish. So I don't see why I couldn't bring home a camel."

"He's got a sister?" Twigs brightened. "I've got a sister too." The galumpus sounded as if he'd just remembered how much he missed her. "Her name is Munch-Munch."

"That's nice."

"She looks up to me," Twigs bragged, but then a shadow crossed his face. Reluctantly, he added, "Sometimes."

"Where's she?" Sparky asked, squirming a bit, maybe

worried that Twigs was about to ask if his sister could come along too.

"With my mom," Twigs said. "I guess."

"You don't know?"

"They're awfully far away."

"That's too bad," Sparky said, sounding relieved. "What do you camels like to eat, anyway?"

"Who?" Twigs asked, briefly forgetting what he was supposed to be, but then he remembered and covered up by saying, "Moss and twigs and stuff. We don't eat a lot."

"Ha," the mayor weighed in. "He hasn't stopped eating since he got here. Look at the size of him."

"You think staying with you might work?" Twigs asked the dog. "I wouldn't take up much room."

"Don't believe him," Sussex warned. "He's just a kid. Hasn't even stopped growing."

"So you say," Sparky said, but after thinking it over a bit, he asked Twigs, "How long would you need to stay?"

"Oh, just a little while. If it will help any, I could give

your family a ride on my back any time they wanted. They might like that."

Without waiting to hear what the dog thought about his offer, Twigs stepped closer to the toboggan. Though nobody bothered to mention it, his lame leg wasn't slowing him down at all. Out stretched his trunk, reaching toward the kids. I'm guessing he wanted to pluck one of them off the toboggan and give them a ride on his back, but it wasn't sound judgment.

For one thing, he already had three of us lined up on his back. Where was he going to put someone else?

On top of which, Twigs was completely forgetting what the 3000 had said about needing to get him home to prevent time rot and inversed ratios and so on.

And last but nowhere near least, he failed to consider what the two kids would think about having a big hairy trunk snaking their way. Hard as they were tugging on their dad's sleeves, they looked as though trying to crawl up his arms. They were yammering about something too. *Dad, we want to go home!* if I had to guess.

Their clamor threw their father into action. With

a yell that didn't sound at all friendly, he tried to push Twigs's trunk away from his kids. He didn't have any luck.

Ruth shouted too—maybe for cooler heads.

"Class!" The 3000 raised her voice. "Please settle down."

The father's shove didn't move Twigs's trunk much, but it was enough to throw the big galumpus off-balance, which made him lose his footing on a slick spot beneath the snow. His front half went whipping one way while his back half slid the other. There's nothing like a patch of ice for speeding things up.

The mayor and Sussex grabbed ahold of the fur on Twigs's back so that they wouldn't get pitched off. Maybe I latched on, too, just a little. When our claws sank in, Twigs reared back in surprise. That's when he really lost his footing, which upset our balance. Not wanting to get thrown off, we grabbed ahold harder, making him thrash about all the more.

I might have caught a whiff of woodsmoke and heard wind chimes for a split second there. It was sort of difficult to tell, what with all the bellowing and thrash-ing going on.

The commotion mushroomed when Twigs bucked us all off. We soared upward together but fell earth-ward separately. Time slowed down the way it does in the movies when something bad is about to happen. Everything stretched out way longer than week-old chewing gum. Dirt with nowhere to go would have moved faster.

At the last second, Twigs twisted away from us and landed with a thud. He bounced the tiniest bit. Barely at all. It turned out that woolly mammoths don't have much bounce in them. And then he thudded down again, this time for good.

Somewhere between Twigs's first and second land-ing, I was pitched into a snowdrift and quit screaming.

After that I definitely heard wind chimes and smelled woodsmoke. Oh yes, the white fog came roll-ing it. I was riding on my mother's back again. All my brothers and sisters were along for the trip. Somehow there was room for the mayor and Sussex, too, along with the 3000 and even the three cavemen with their club, mop, and spear.

The only ones who hadn't come along were the man in the red-checkered cap, his children, the small white dog named Sparky, and Twigs.

"What's that?" one of my brothers asked, pointing at the sky.

Looking up, I saw the toboggan soaring above us. Twigs was steering it, searching for a place to land on my mother's back.

I cupped my paws around my mouth and called up to him: "There's no room."

The big galumpus took the news awful personal. The way his face crimped up and he started bawling was a sight to behold. Teardrops were plummeting. They whistled like dropping bombs. A gigantic one drenched me, and I nearly drowned. Good thing the white fog started to break apart before another tear hit me. My mother waddled away, carrying off everyone but me. That didn't leave me much choice but to quit playing dead. Someone was yanking on my ear.

Chapter 28

A Volunteer

The mayor was telling me it was time to go. He and Sussex were about to sneak out the back side of the snowdrift where we'd all been pitched.

"What about Twigs?" I asked.

"After saying we'd kidnapped him? He's on his own."

"He's only making things up because he's desperate," I said. "He's just a kid, and you know we're honor bound to help him."

They didn't take kindly to being reminded of that.

"All he has to do is follow the dern street," the mayor groused. "It'll take him straight to the creek. He and that hotshot bear ought to be able to handle that much, don't you think? They've got the girl to help them too."

"But what if they run into something they need us for?" I asked.

"Like what?" Sussex squawked. "You want us to take care of that galumpus till we're old and gray?"

"No," I told them, doing my best to stay calm, "I just want to make sure he gets home so that everything and everyone ends up back where they belong."

"Everyone?" the mayor crabbed. "Who's everyone?"

"How about those cavemen?" I reminded them. "Don't we have to do something about them too? Unless you want them running around the park trying to spear you for years and years."

A thought like that left them mumbling, but at least they stuck around.

As for Twigs, he'd fallen on his side when he'd lost his balance. His left rear leg was bent crookedly beneath him. That didn't look good. That didn't look good at all.

"Don't touch me!" he cried, sounding as if he hurt from the tip of trunk to the end of his tail. "Don't!"

This time I'd say he really *had* hurt something.

"We have got to get him moving," the 3000 said once I described Twigs's position.

"Just leave me here," Twigs begged.

"You know we can't," the 3000 said.

"I'll be fine," Twigs promised. "Sparky's invited me to stay with his family."

"That's right," Sparky agreed. "He doesn't look in any condition to be traveling. Just let me tell my people he's coming with us."

At which point Sparky did a whole lot of barking and prancing around in front of his family, acting as if they'd know exactly what he meant. In my experience, dogs have convinced themselves of the most ridiculous kind of piffle when it comes to the people they live with. I didn't for a minute believe his family was going to open their front door and welcome Twigs in. For starters, he might not have fit through it. And the way that family was watching in disbelief as Sparky whirled around them? I sure didn't think they'd understood a single word of what he was carrying on about. Desperate as they called to him and tried to catch him, they seemed to think they were saving him from us.

"They're thinking it over," Sparky reported before launching into a whole new batch of *woof*s and *arf*s that only made his family try all the harder to grab him.

"Class," the 3000 announced while that was going on, "I may need your assistance with Twigs."

With much pushing and shoving and coaxing and wheedling, we somehow got Twigs back on his feet. The 3000 and Ruth did most of the work, but I pitched in where I could. The mayor and Sussex limited themselves to making terrible threats about what would happen to Twigs if he didn't get up.

"I don't care," Twigs bleated. "I just don't care."

"You will if those cavemen get ahold of you."

Even so, Twigs didn't help at all. And once we had him on his feet, he teetered and wobbled and whimpered as if he might collapse. This time that leg of his was really, truly in bad shape.

Having a brainstorm, I said, "What about the toboggan?"

"What about it?" the mayor snapped.

"We could use it to pull Twigs."

"Who's strong enough to do that?" the mayor demanded to know.

"That galumpus isn't exactly light," Sussex piled on. Nothing perked that red squirrel up like a chance to knock down something I'd suggested.

"Class," the 3000 spoke up, "I should have sufficient power for that task, if someone can lead me in the right direction."

"Now, hold everything," the mayor objected. "What about your precious time line? Won't borrowing that toboggan contaminate it?"

"Taking the toboggan results in a lower probability of a cross-time infection than being trapped here," the 3000 answered. "We shall have to risk it."

"All right," the mayor caved, forced to see her point.

"I guess Gilly can handle being your eyes. We all know how bad he's always wanting to be up front."

Now, that was pure Mayor Crawdaddy through and through. Volunteer you for a terrible job and act like he was doing you a favor at the same time. Sussex didn't disappoint either.

"Aren't you going to be up there with him, Crawdaddy?" the Earl of Sussex asked.

Cornered, the mayor had no choice but to crossly say, "Well of course I am. Somebody's got to make sure he doesn't faint."

The two of them were so busy going after each other that I never got an opening to stand up for myself and say I wasn't planning on doing any fainting if I could help it. They kept at it until Ruth volunteered to be the 3000's eyes, which settled everything. Or almost. The 3000 still had to tell the people that we were commandeering their toboggan in the name of the Theodore Wirth Wildlife and Time Preservation Sanctuary. Just hearing a green bear speak convinced the father to scoop up his kids, one under each arm, and escape into the blizzard, leaving the toboggan behind.

"Maybe another time," Sparky told Twigs before racing after his family.

The big galumpus tried following the dog for a step and a half before crumpling to the ground in pain. That leg of his was worthless.

Chapter 29

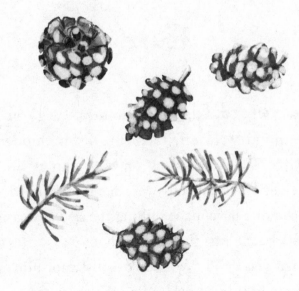

Found

Fast as we could, we crammed Twigs onto the toboggan and were off, following Ruth through the snowdrifts. Twigs ended up on his rump at the back of the sled. His haunches were hanging off the sides, which couldn't have made pulling the sled any easier for the 3000, but at least the big galumpus was facing to the rear. That was good. We didn't really want him seeing how the lightning and thunder up ahead seemed to be smashing the whole world to bits.

"Are you sure about this?" the mayor called out to the 3000.

He, Sussex, and I were riding at the front of the toboggan, able to see where we were headed.

"Class," the 3000 patiently answered, "the atmospheric activity you are probably seeing means we are headed in the right direction. Conditions around a time tunnel can be turbulent, especially when the tunnel starts to degrade."

"What's that mean?" I asked.

"That we're running out of time."

"What are you talking about up there?" Twigs asked,

trying not to squirm. Moving made his twisted leg hurt all the more.

"How pretty everything looks," Sussex told him.

"Ain't pretty as home," Twigs mumbled to himself. After a minute, he added bitterly, "But I guess it'll have to do."

"Oh no it won't," the mayor told him. "You're going home."

"But I could never leave all the friends I've made here," Twigs mocked.

His tone made it clear that his feelings had been hurt by how fast we were trying to ship him off.

"We've been doing our best to help you," I said. Or at least some of us had.

"By sending me home? Some help."

The mayor and Sussex glanced away when he delivered that. On a misty night you might have almost mistaken them for someone feeling guilty.

"Everybody's treated me so swell," Twigs bitterly moped on, meaning exactly the opposite. "I don't know how I could ever just up and leave after all the wonderful things that you've done for me. It just wouldn't be right."

"You're going home," the mayor vowed, unfazed by the sarcasm.

The blunt words shut the big galumpus down for a few seconds, but only a few, after which came an outburst: "I wish I could!"

When I asked why in the world he couldn't, Twigs went quiet as an empty culvert. He even quit moaning about how his leg hurt. Something about the prospect of going home tore him up awfully bad.

We had other problems too.

The 3000 was flickering more and more. All her creaking and clacking and whirring made it sound as if she had a bad case of indigestion, even though she probably didn't even have a stomach. And every once in a while I caught a whiff of hot oil lifting off her, as if she might be overheating. But then again, although fallen snow melted and glistened on her green fur, her smushed hat had a halo of white snow all the way around its brim. That hadn't been here before and made me think that parts of her were running cold. When we started out, she paused every tenth step to give her batteries a rest. Within a block she barely made it seven steps before needing to stop. Still, she did her best to keep us motivated.

"Class," she said over her shoulder, hesitating as if she'd misplaced what she wanted to say, "you shall all go down in . . ." Another pause. ". . . park history as heroes. Your actions will preserve the time line that allows the sanctuary and time preserve to exist."

"Whoopee," the mayor grumbled, which just went to show how bad off we were. Most days he liked flattery better than swiped eggs.

"You'll be written up extensively," the 3000 assured him. "Generations of schoolchildren will read about your valor during the blizzard of 2023."

"Any statues of us?" the mayor asked.

There were some bronze statues of people in the park that the mayor was fond of sniffing around in the wee hours. Many's the time I'd found him admiring them before calling it a night and heading back to his den.

Where the mayor went, the Earl of Sussex wasn't far behind.

"Statues of all of us?" the red squirrel clarified.

"Not yet," the 3000 said after some whirring inside

her. "But I shall definitely put in a recommendation for their . . . construction after all you've done . . . today."

A distant wailing put an end to all talk of statues. Falling snow muffled the sound, which seemed vaguely familiar, as if I'd heard it before, but it faded away before I could remember where.

"Now what?" groaned the mayor, shooting me a look.

At first I thought it might be the cavemen howling, though that didn't make sense, for the sound came from in front of us. So far as I knew, the cavemen were tagging along to the rear, licking their wounds after battling the leaf blower.

The wailing wasn't shrill like the ambulances or fire trucks or police sirens that sometimes tore past the park. It wobbled, almost squeaked, sounding forlorn, maybe lost. What if it was coming from the time tunnel? What if we were all about to be sucked into the distant past? Or flung into the unknowable future? I found myself being way more attached to the here and now than I'd ever noticed before. It was where I belonged and was known and had family, and maybe more important, where I was needed. I wasn't feeling at all eager to go trading all that in for some time where they might not even know about things like cupcakes and potato chips. In short, I was getting a taste of the kind of troubles that must have been ripping Twigs apart.

And all the while I was working up a sweat about that, the sound crept closer, fading in and out on the wind. Each new wail brought us to a standstill.

"Now what?" griped the mayor.

"Class," the 3000 said, "I'm afraid the sound does not match any . . . entries currently accessible in my database."

"Well, isn't that just dandy?" sniped the Earl of Sussex.

The mayor wasn't shy about spreading his unhappiness around, either, but the new sound seemed to perk up Ruth. Stopping, she cupped her hands around her mouth and shouted *Hoo!* Whatever was out there answered with a wavery cry.

"Is she trying to talk to that thing?" sputtered the mayor. "Tell her to knock it off! Who knows what it is!"

The 3000 passed that on to Ruth, who answered right away.

"She says . . . you don't need to worry," the 3000 said.

"You tell her that I'll do all the worrying I want," Crawdaddy came back.

While they straightened that out, whatever was calling to Ruth kept on getting closer, and clearer, and more urgent. It seemed to be headed straight for us. I decided it sounded like a car horn, which brought to mind the snowplow that had tried to run us over.

"Might be a good time to get off the street," I suggested.

"Is that your answer for everything?" grouched the mayor. To Twigs, he said, "You, galumpus. Ever heard this kind of beast before?"

"Ah, no?"

"Hoo!" Ruth again called out.

"That's enough!" Crawdaddy shouted at her.

As the wails drew nearer, and louder, the snow tumbling down in front of us started to change color to a bedazzling white. Any other time, I would have applauded the show, but at the moment I was agonizing about how much light a time tunnel might throw off.

In between the wails, I began to hear something

crunching through the snow. It wasn't the left-right, left-right tromp of heavy feet. It sounded more like wheels that were slowly rolling our way. The 3000 hadn't mentioned whether time tunnels could move around, but then again, I hadn't asked.

A pair of angry eyes glared through the blizzard. Dim at first, they grew brighter fast. There wasn't any blink to them, either. Being studied by eyes like that was far more uncomfortable than being looked over by the single eye of Birdy's snowblower. I started wondering what else from the distant past or far-flung future might have gotten tossed into the park, and what kind of costumes they might be wearing, and if they expected their young'uns to collect tusks. Most anything was starting to seem possible in this storm. And naturally I was curious as to whether this latest set of eyes might have any kind of sweet tooth for woolly mammoths or raccoons or red squirrels or, yes, I'll admit it, possums.

Falling snow cloaked most of the beast, though there might have been some eyebrows twitching wicked-like above the eyes. And it could have totally been my imagination getting carried away, but I saw the outline of a hungry mouth below those eyes.

At least we could quit wondering where the wailing was coming from.

I caught the mayor casting about for the handiest way to bail out, and the Earl of Sussex ducked below the toboggan's curved front. I hunched down with him.

Somewhere in there Ruth quit guiding us forward.

The beast stopped too. Its wail went away. The slow, rolling crunch of snow it had been making was replaced by a ticking sound. I got to thinking that maybe this thing in front of us was trying to clear its throat of a bone that had gotten stuck while gobbling up the last stranger it'd met.

We faced off that way for a good ten thousand years, neither side budging, until Twigs, who was still riding backward on the sled and couldn't see what we'd come up against, bawled out, "What if they don't want me back?"

That popped out of him so unexpectedly that nobody, not even Sussex, knew what to say. For someone who claimed he didn't want to go home, he sounded pretty shook up about what they might be thinking of him back there. The outburst made Ruth concerned enough to ask the 3000 what the problem was, but before the green bear could answer, Twigs cried out a second time.

"They probably haven't even noticed I'm gone!"

There wasn't any chance to comfort him, either. Right then the beast before us wailed one last time. Its sound seemed more familiar than ever, though, rattled as I was, I couldn't place from where until the sound ended and a human voice hailed us.

"Ruth?"

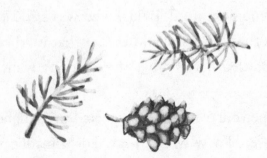

Chapter 30

Cavemen to the Rescue?

My head popped up above the toboggan's curled front. The burning eyes I'd been hiding from? They turned out to be headlights on a car big enough to bull through the snow.

A car door opened and Ruth's brother leaned out. His thin mustache and hat with earflaps gave him away. Ruth may not have been old enough to drive, but it appeared he was. The wailing we'd heard had come from his trumpet, still in his hand. He'd been calling Ruth to him.

With a shout, Ruth rushed forward, so glad to see her brother, she nearly knocked him over. Tight as she hugged him? He nearly lost his stuffing. Something told me that Ruth had been putting on a brave front for our benefit. All the time she'd been helping us, she must have secretly been asking herself, *What am I doing? What am I doing? What am I doing?*

The reunion didn't last long. Her brother appeared to be more relieved than overjoyed to have found her. Holding her at arm's length, he proceeded to chew her out but good. His tone said, *What were you thinking? What were you thinking? What were you thinking?*

To which Ruth soon fired back in a tone that said, *I told you that Gilly needed help! What did you expect me to do! He could have frozen to death!*

"Who's this guy?" asked the mayor.

"Her brother," I said.

"He doesn't sound happy," Sussex added.

"What's going on?" Twigs complained, still facing the wrong way to see for himself.

"Ruth's brother has found us," I said.

"Has he come for me?" Twigs asked, both excited and scared.

"Let's hope so." A cheap shot from Sussex.

"Class," the 3000 chided. "Our respectful hats, please."

By then the brother had gotten a load of us, and a serious frown wrinkled his forehead. Untangling himself from his sister, he edged back toward his car door, moving as if crossing thin ice. His steps had good-sized pauses in between them. If he was dawdling in hopes of reinforcements, I didn't hear any other trumpets blowing in the distance. Pointing our way, he spoke loudly. I'd heard people use that booming kind of voice before, usually when ordering me to stand back and not come any closer. Wild shooing motions usually went with the warning.

"He's telling us to leave," the 3000 passed on, "and not to try any funny business."

"What's funny business?" Twigs asked.

"Anything that's not funny," I told him.

"That don't sound right," Twigs said. "What's that thing he's holding?"

"His trumpet," I answered. "It makes that wailing sound we've been hearing."

"Naw," Twigs disputed, refusing to believe me.

"I'm with the galumpus on that one," Mayor Crawdaddy said. "That thing doesn't look big enough to make such a racket."

Unwilling to look away from us, Ruth's brother asked her a question out the side of his mouth while protecting his trumpet by pressing it against his chest.

"He wants to know if we're from a circus," the 3000 relayed to the rest of us.

"Who else would have us?" the mayor muttered.

"What'd Ruth tell him?" I asked, trying to get the mayor's mind off being slighted. Nothing good had ever come of his feeling that way.

"I'm afraid she lied and said we were from a circus," the 3000 said. "She said we were trying . . . to find our way home."

"Don't say that word!" Twigs blurted, twisting about so fast that he nearly tipped the toboggan over.

Much bellowing and threatening followed until Twigs righted himself and the toboggan settled back down. Once we'd all calmed a bit, Ruth's brother unleashed several questions that kept Ruth busy answering. You could tell they were arguing.

"He wants to know," the 3000 told us, "where we got the toboggan and how Ruth met up with a furry elephant and a green bear."

"I'd like to know the answers to that!" Sussex spoke up.

"Class," the 3000 warned. "Best behavior, please . . . while I try to explain our situation."

We quieted down to let her try, but being addressed by a green bear didn't improve the brother's mood. In fact, he was looking more distrustful and headachy by the second. His hand holding the trumpet had begun to tremble.

"Gilly," the mayor said while that was going on, "I'm thinking we have done about all that can be expected on behalf of the animals of Theodore Wirth Park."

"Above and beyond, I'd say," Sussex promptly agreed.

"Maybe above and beyond is what's called for," I pointed out, sorely disappointed in both of them.

"And," the mayor plunged on, "I'm thinking we should turn the galumpus and green bear over to these two people. They look plenty capable to me. I'm sure they'll figure out what to do with them."

"What about the cavemen?" I asked again, just to bedevil him.

"They can feel free to worry about them, too."

From time to time it fell to me to remind the mayor of his better self. It was as nasty a job as ever was, and I was sorely tempted to pass on it. I'd never before gotten so much as a thank-you for taking it on. Sour looks and snide comments were the usual payment.

And the snow kept on falling.

And my fur was getting wetter.

And my nose colder.

And Twigs asked, "Do you think they'd take me home with them?"

But sometimes all the excuses and interruptions in the world can't save you from having to do something.

And catching sight of Twigs at the back of the tobog-gan, all alone and snivelly and about as far from home as he could be—even if he claimed he didn't want to go there—seeing him there reminded me that Crawdaddy had taken an oath when he agreed to be mayor. That oath included upholding park rules and ethics, such as helping fellow animals in need. Getting a job as big as that done wasn't always going to be easy. And I'd gotten hitched up to the same duties and responsibilities when I'd signed on to be his assistant. For crying out loud, I'd never be able to live with myself, or all my brothers and sisters and cousins and neighbors, if I didn't say some-thing.

"How do we know," I said to the mayor and Sussex, "that Ruth and her brother will be able to get the big galumpus and the 3000 to that tunnel in time?"

The mayor didn't take kindly to anyone bringing up a thought as pesky as that. He particularly didn't appre-ciate my speaking up in the middle of a blizzard that was keeping him from a warm den. It appeared his bet-ter self wasn't going to be putting in an appearance any time soon.

"Nobody asked for your two cents!" the mayor raged.

"Of all the ungrateful—" Sussex chipped in, even more outraged.

"They probably wouldn't mind if I stayed with them for a while," Twigs offered. "You know, like the hamster and goldfish those little kids had."

"Class," the 3000 said, interrupting our squabble, "I've clarified to Ruth's brother that we're more time travelers than circus performers. I've explained that Twigs is not a furry elephant but a woolly mammoth. And he now knows that I'm an educational robot, not a . . . bear. Finally, I've done my best to impress upon him the importance of getting Twigs back to his own time, and that to do that we need to reach a time tunnel caused by this storm, a tunnel that's probably degrading . . . as we speak."

"You and that time tunnel," griped the mayor.

"Told you, I ain't going," Twigs said.

"What'd he say to all that?" I asked, doing my best to keep the discussion moving along.

"That he needs to get his sister home before their parents get back or he'll be in deep trouble."

"Deeper trouble than losing our time line?" the mayor demanded, doing a sudden about-face on how important that was.

"He also says," the 3000 continued, "that we're almost to the creek and should be able to make it the rest of the way without them."

"Now, that's just lazy," the mayor scoffed, conveniently forgetting that barely a minute ago he'd been about to push the same job off on them.

"To say nothing of ungrateful," fumed Sussex, "after all that we've done to try to save this time line."

"What's Ruth say?" I asked.

"That their parents would want them to help us," the 3000 said.

I didn't get a chance to agree with that. Twigs spoke up first.

"You can tell her," the big galumpus burst in, sounding as though he'd had plenty of experience with parents, "to forget that!"

"I'm not sure that's the best message to share," the 3000 cautioned.

"All right," Twigs huffed, having heard enough, "I'll tell her."

With that, the big galumpus struggled to his feet, which took some serious grunting and whimpering and blowing. His injured leg had stiffened up since we'd sat him down on the toboggan and was paining him worse than ever. Yet he managed to get himself upright, even if only standing on three legs. That was when Ruth's brother got his first full look at Twigs's size and staggered backward a step.

"It doesn't matter what she thinks her parents would tell her," Twigs lashed out. "She can't trust them. Parents will tell you anything to get you to do what *they* think is best. Anything. And if she thinks they ever want her to grow up and do anything on her own, or discover anything new, or go around with anyone interesting, or have any fun—any fun at all—or make friends, or taste something good—forget it! Just forget it.

"And her mother sure won't listen to anything she has to say. Forget that, too. Mothers ain't interested in what you've got to say, only in what you hear, so long as what you hear is coming from them.

"And fathers ain't any better. Not at all. So far as a father cares, you're nothing but a pair of ears to shout at. And the same goes for any grown-up in your whole herd. And she better not go pretending that her brother will take her side. A brother or sister will go blabbing everything you tell them straight to your mother or father or whoever. Why? 'Cause tattling on you is the only way they'll ever get anyone to listen to them about anything. In the end, you're on your own. You tell her that!"

The big galumpus was so totally worked up that he completely forgot that Ruth and her brother couldn't understand a single word of what he was blathering. He might as well have been shouting at a cliff or a stop sign or an empty hole in the ground. They would have understood him just as well and been only slightly less stupefied.

What saved him from figuring out what a fool he was making of himself? The way the three cavemen came charging out of the blizzard. Why, it was almost as if they were coming to his rescue.

Chapter 31

The Earl of Sussex Has an Idea

Those cavemen had gone and plundered another house. Wolf-head was holding a framed picture of a golden sunset in front of himself as if it was a shield.

Saber-tooth had proudly tucked a chrome toaster under his arm. When he thought no one was looking, he sneaked peeks at his reflection in the toaster's side. He'd also collected a sky-blue towel that he'd draped over his shoulders to help keep warm. By then icicles dangled from his hair and his soaked animal skins were stiff as boards.

As for Boar-head, he'd latched on to a green golf bag that was stuffed full of clubs. It clashed with the lampshade he was still wearing, but he didn't seem to mind. He'd yet to figure out that the bag had a shoulder strap, and used both hands to carry it. Every few feet he had to set it down to rest his arms. That gave him a chance to admire the green mask they'd taken from Birdy. It now covered the top of one of the golf clubs, looking inscrutable.

They weren't shouting any less either. This time around, the 3000 didn't bother filling us in on their threats.

"Class," the 3000 called out, "stay together, please."

To which the Earl of Sussex said, "I'm no expert, but won't staying together make it easier for them to catch us?"

"Feel free to take 'em on all by yourself," the mayor instructed.

Thank goodness it didn't come to that. Ruth's brother was more comfortable dealing with painted men dressed up in animal skins than with possums and galumpuses and robots and such.

He got their attention by lifting the trumpet to his lips and blowing hard enough to make nearby pines sway, or so it seemed. The mayor, Sussex, and Twigs developed a sudden respect for the horn. The cavemen were dumbfounded.

A single, clear note rang out, making the snow dancing in the headlights quiver. I doubt that a knock on the head would have stunned those cavemen any more than the brassy sound of that horn. They groveled as if they'd never heard anything so incredible. When Ruth's brother paused for a breath and the note faded, the cavemen shouted for more, or at least that's what the 3000 said they were saying. Ruth's brother obliged. That trumpet was the only thing keeping the cavemen at bay.

Eventually, Boar-head got over his astonishment. Setting his golf bag down, he lifted a club out of the bag and hefted it as if trying to decide whether it was the right weight for the job. He also ordered Wolf-head and Saber-tooth to fan out and surround Ruth's brother, or at least I guessed that's what all his shouting and hand-waving was about. The way their eyes stayed glued to that trumpet? They must have been thinking they'd found a secret weapon that would make rivers flow backward.

Saber-tooth slunk off to the left, setting his toaster aside real careful-like to free up his hands. Reluctantly, he shed the blue towel from his shoulders.

Wolf-head seemed reborn now that he was protected by that sunset painting. Acting invincible, he went straight at Ruth's brother.

Seeing what they were up to, Twigs trumpeted at them loud enough to knock snow off branches, I swear, but just then the cavemen weren't paying him any mind. They only had eyes for the trumpet. Ruth's brother retreated toward the car, sounding his horn as he went.

Boar-head advanced with an outstretched hand, talking every step of the way. Soothingly as he spoke, he must have been trying to coax Ruth's brother into handing over his trumpet. Saber-tooth hung back, wanting nothing to do with the horn. But Wolf-head went so far as to offer up one of the shrunken roots from his necklace, willing to make a trade.

Ruth's brother refused their offers. Between blowing on the trumpet and screaming at his sister to get in the car, he was out of breath. With his free hand, he opened a rear car door and waved wildly for Ruth to jump in the car.

Ruth had other ideas. Veterinarians didn't abandon their patients. Helping Twigs meant getting the 3000 moving again, so she yelled and shook the robot by the shoulders, bringing her around briefly. The green bear teetered a few steps before losing power and grinding to a new halt.

As for the cavemen . . . they were so keen on getting the trumpet that they never even noticed that reinforcements had arrived.

To be fair, none of us noticed.

But help was on the way.

With a wild battle cry, Birdy came charging out of the storm. He'd picked up a limp, lost his green mask, and had silver duct tape holding together his light sword as well as patching a gash on the top of his bald head. Yet he was gallant as ever. He rushed past the cavemen and the toboggan, grabbed Ruth's hand before she knew what was happening, and swept her toward the car. She tried yanking herself free, without luck.

Birdy and Ruth's brother had joined forces and were both pulling her to safety. Together they managed to stuff her inside the car. Of course the cavemen were having none of that. But Birdy held them off with screams and several serious swipes of his light sword. A couple of trumpet blasts slowed them down further, giving Birdy and the brother time to leap into the car themselves.

My, how those cavemen howled when the car doors slammed shut in their faces! They swarmed the car's hood, beating on the windshield and doors and tires and bumpers and a dozen other places I didn't know the name of. That car's windows were made of sturdy glass! Those cavemen only got winded trying to smash them. They barely managed to put a few cracks in them, which drove them all the wilder, especially when Ruth's brother started honking the car horn. They jumped straight into the air when that happened.

Leaping off the hood, they retreated, covering their ears and doubling over, but they soon enough got ahold of themselves and came charging back, wanting that trumpet worse than ever. The way they were yelling and carrying on, I'm surprised their tongues didn't fall out.

In the middle of all that, the Earl of Sussex had himself an idea, and for once it wasn't pure flapdoodle. This time around he came up with something worth listening to.

"What are we waiting for?" Sussex called out. "Let's get out of here!"

"Class," the 3000 said, barely whirring back to life, "I'm afraid my optical sensors . . . remain offline."

"Gilly!" the mayor yelled. "Help the robot!"

"With what?"

"Your eyes. What'd you think?"

For a split second I nearly said *Do it yourself,* but we didn't have the time to bicker. Standing, I climbed atop the toboggan's curled front and leaped for the 3000's back. Nobody ever expects possums to be leapers, but hanging out in trees teaches you things. I landed on her shoulders with a thump that jarred the 3000 to life. The green fur on her neck was all rubbery and slick from melted snow and nearly impossible to hold on to, even when your life depended on it.

"Hurry up," the mayor ordered.

"He's hopeless," Sussex added.

"What about me?" Twigs bleated from the back of the toboggan.

"Class," the 3000 weakly announced, "I'm sure Gilly is doing . . . the best he can."

"He better be," warned the mayor.

Once perched on the 3000's shoulders, I didn't even take time to catch my breath, but gasped, "Go right."

And right we went, plunging into the storm. We left the rampaging cavemen and honking car behind. The last I saw of Ruth, she was waving for us to go faster, a suggestion that I passed on to the 3000, for all the good it did. That robot's power was dwindling fast as a star's twinkle at dawn.

Chapter 32

Lightening the Load

Being the eyes for a robot whose power kept cutting out wasn't any picnic. The herky-jerky way she lurched forward nearly pitched me off her shoulders. I had to wrap my front paws around her neck, cram my nose behind her ear, and hang on for dear life. Clinging that close to her filled my nose with an oily smell that had my stomach flip-flopping. And the nearer we got to the creek, the deeper the snowdrifts, the heavier the snowfall, the gaudier the lightning. At times the whole sky seemed on fire.

If Twigs hadn't been constantly moaning about his leg and not wanting to go home, and complaining about having snow packed up his trunk, I'd have devoted some time to worrying about how Ruth and her brother and Birdy were holding up behind us. As it was, I spent most of my spare energy yelling back at Twigs to hang in there. I told him that no matter what he thought, I was pretty sure his mother wanted him to come home. When that didn't help, I went into how my brothers and sisters were big tattletales, too, and that he was lucky to have a father who showed up long enough to shout at him. Possum fathers never did.

None of it did any good. He kept right on finding reasons to stay with us.

"Something's always burning back there," he said, to which I couldn't think of a single thing to say. Talking about woodsmoke always left me uneasy for personal reasons.

Meanwhile, the mayor and Sussex peered over the

toboggan's curled front. About the only thing they seemed to see through their iced-up whiskers and eyelashes was doom. I surely didn't care for the way the two of them put their heads together to plot.

In short, we were all one big, happy family.

The only one not complaining was the 3000. She seemed to be conserving energy by keeping her mouth shut.

But wait, there was one slim little ray of hope that our trials and tribulations might be reaching an end, if we survived long enough. The street we were following soon led us back to an arm of Theodore Wirth. No matter how much the mayor and Sussex muttered, we were making progress. We re-entered the park near a community garden I'd been known to visit. If we stuck around for six months, we might have heard radishes calling to us, but at the moment all those seeds were beneath a thick blanket of snow, dreaming of April showers. Beyond the covered garden was a line of trees that marked the banks of Bassett Creek. We were getting close.

Except that now a new problem reared its head.

The wind picked up, battering us and making it even harder for the 3000 to keep going. By the time we reached the line of trees, the robot had to rest after every fourth step. Pressing an ear against her furry neck, I couldn't hear much of anything going on inside her. Shouldn't there have at least been some buzzing or fizzing?

"Now what?" Crawdaddy squawked during one rest stop.

"Class," the 3000 weakly answered, "the time vortex must be . . . getting closer."

"The what?"

"The time vortex. The opening to the time anomaly that . . . brought us here. What Twigs calls . . . a cave. I fear it's draining my batteries faster than I . . . anticipated."

"Great," the mayor griped.

"Any other surprises you want to share?" Sussex asked.

"Class, your patience hats . . . please. I shall need a few extra moments to let my batteries recharge."

"Take all the time you want," said Twigs. "I'm not going into that cave again, no matter what you call it."

"Really now," I cajoled, "don't you want to go home at all?"

"Never," the big galumpus sniveled.

"Like it or not, you're going," the mayor told him. "We didn't come all this way just to keep you around to eat us out of prairie and woods."

"And contaminate our time line," Sussex added.

Our family was getting happier by the second. But finally the 3000's batteries had stored enough energy for us to push onward. I guided the 3000 to a wide footbridge over the creek, whose dark waters were swollen by all the snow the storm was dumping into it. Visibility was so sketchy that I could barely see across the bridge. All I could make out on the far side was enough lightning flashes and thunder rumblings to make me wonder if the mayor might relent and decide that Twigs better stay with us after all. But no, his mind was made up.

"Keep moving," he ordered.

The 3000 flickered every step of the way across the footbridge. She was crackling regularly too. Once, she blacked out entirely, locked right in place. That set the mayor and Sussex off, but before they could do anything drastic, I grabbed a paw full of green fur and yanked. The 3000 stirred with a feeble click.

On the far side of the creek the wind rushed through tree branches. A stiff breeze now pelted our faces with snow that was leaning toward sleet.

"What's that?" Twigs gasped.

"What's what?" the mayor grouched, sounding about as close to the end of his rope as he could get without running out of rope.

"I smell home!" Twigs bawled, forgetting for an instant that he didn't want anything to do with that place.

Sniffing, I couldn't believe my nose. The wind blowing in our faces carried a strong whiff of summer grass and pond scum and basking turtles. How'd that get all mixed up with ice and snow?

"We're getting close," the 3000 announced, raising her voice to be heard above the wind. "You're probably smelling . . . debris blown through the tunnel from the other side, where it's summer."

"How close?" Twigs sounded torn in half.

"I'm thinking we're not going to make it," the mayor said.

"Seems doubtful," Sussex seconded.

"Class," the 3000 said, "it's the vortex that's increasing the wind, but I calculate that I should have enough . . . power to get us there."

"I've had about enough of your calculations," the mayor called out. "Maybe it's time to lighten the load."

"What are you talking about?" I shouted, though I had a notion of exactly what he was talking about—getting back to his cozy den.

"This toboggan's too heavy," the mayor answered. "That poor bear can hardly pull it. The least we can do is make her job easier."

"How?" A sick feeling was rising fast inside me.

"By making the load lighter," the mayor answered. Turning all noble, he hurried to add, "Don't you worry about me. I might freeze to death in a snowbank, or get run through by a spear, but that's all right. If that's the sacrifice I have to make to help this poor lost galumpus get back to his ma, then I know it's worth it."

His voice modestly trailed off. What rot! He was terrified about getting closer to the vortex, that's all. The Earl of Sussex joined the mayor on the spot.

"I'd better go with him," the red squirrel chimed in. "To help make the load even lighter."

The coward! Even wet he didn't weigh much more than a paw full of dandelion fluff. Taken together, the two of them wouldn't have outweighed a pumpkin.

Sacrifice themselves? Total rubbish! They were out to save their skins, but before I could call them on it, Twigs came to life, nearly climbing off the toboggan.

"Is that Ma?" the young woolly asked, sounding spooked. He flapped his furry ears as if someone was calling to him.

He had better hearing than me. All I caught was the wind whipping around us, snapping off branches and sweeping them to the ends of the world.

"Don't you worry," the mayor yelled to Twigs at the back of the toboggan. "You still got Gilly. He ought to be better than nothing."

And with that the mayor pinched his nose and

flipped backward off the toboggan, into the snow. The Earl of Sussex didn't waste any time joining him.

"You will be remembered!" the red squirrel called out to me before bailing out.

The last I saw of those two, they were getting blown back across the footbridge, merging into all the white.

"Quitters!" I screamed after them, for all the good it did. The wind drowned me out.

I halfway expected Twigs to go limping after them, dead set as he was against going home, but he stayed planted on the back of the toboggan. He glanced over his shoulder at me, as if expecting me to say something hearty and courageous. Well, I gave it my best shot.

"Better hold on" was all I could come up with.

Chapter 33

A Poor Junior Possum

"Class?" the 3000 called out, maybe wondering if everyone had abandoned her.

Through still clinging to the robot's shoulders, I didn't answer. I was gazing too hard at the spot where the mayor and Sussex had disappeared into the blizzard. Speech was beyond me.

It was a long shot, but I was praying that the mayor and Sussex would have a change of heart and come slinking back. I was sincerely hoping that I wasn't the only one left to help the 3000 get Twigs home. I'm ashamed to admit it, but a job that size had me wondering if there wasn't a whiff of woodsmoke tickling my nose. Playing dead was looking better by the second.

But no matter how hard I strained, not a whiff or tinkle came my way. Even my ability to play dead had left me. All I got were those summer smells I've already mentioned, and they weren't comforting at all, not even to Twigs.

"Ain't going home," the big galumpus reminded us.

Hearing that again slammed me back into the here and the now. And if anywhere could have left me colder and more lonesome than this here and this now, I had never been there before.

"Class?" the 3000 repeated.

I wish that I could say that I rose to the occasion. That in that time of troubles I saw what needed doing and found the courage to do it. That's not what happened, though. Instead of brave, I got angry. Overheated angry. I found myself muttering about what a raw deal I was getting.

Was this blizzard my fault? No, one possum couldn't have caused any weather even close to it. Why, I'd never even been able to convince a single, measly cloud to blot out the sun on a hot summer day.

Was it my fault that a time tunnel had opened up to the distant past? No way. It wasn't as if I'd been fooling around with time and caused it. I didn't even own a clock. What possum would? When I'd woken up that morning, I hadn't even known that such things as time vortexes and inverse time-ratio paradoxes existed.

Was it my fault that this young galumpus had wandered into the time tunnel, ended up in our park, and now didn't want to go back where he belonged? I don't see how anyone with any sense could pin that on me either.

Or the cavemen, or the 3000, or the way that Mayor Crawdaddy and the Earl of Sussex had left us—none of it was my fault. Not a bit.

And yet here I was, stuck with trying to take care of all of it.

"What?" I snapped at the 3000.

"Which way should I go?" the 3000 asked.

I almost said, *How should I know? Go whichever way you want. You're the hotshot from the future. I'm nothing but a poor junior possum who'd rather be riding on his mother's back with all his brothers and sisters than getting blown all over the park in this storm.*

In the midst of me lining up all the things I ought to have said, Twigs shared a familiar line.

"Not home," he said again. "Ain't going that way."

Except that this time it came out of him more flimsy than stubborn.

Something about the way he said it reminded me of my own voice. I mean the pathetic one shuffling around in the back of my head. The whiny one that was going on about how unfair everything was. Maybe me and that galumpus were two peas in a pod right on down the line, except for one little thing. My home was considerably closer than Twigs's.

Think that didn't leave me feeling sheepish? Right then was when I knew that if I ever hoped to hold my head up high again, I was going to have to quit feeling sorry for myself, and quit complaining about how rough I had it, and do everything I could to help this poor galumpus out.

"Class," the 3000 reminded us, "we're running out of . . . time."

"Go straight," I said, managing to scrounge up a smidgen of courage from somewhere or other.

So onward we trudged, reaching the far side of the bridge and a blacktop bike path that led away from it. You couldn't see the path beneath the snowdrifts, but I knew from past adventures that it was there, headed toward a highway that cut through Theodore Wirth.

Around a bend the wind howled louder than ever. The 3000 had to crawl on all fours to make any head-way at all. I had to cling as close to her as I could or risk getting blown back to the creek. The shine of her fur dulled. Several times she stopped in midcrawl as if having lost all power. And when starting up again, she was always slower than before.

The smaller trees around us had been snapped in half. Brush had been stripped completely away, but the scent of summer kept growing stronger. The rumbling of thunder got so bad that it shook my whiskers *and* my teeth.

In the middle of all that, Twigs bellowed something that left me not knowing whether to laugh or cry.

"The cave!"

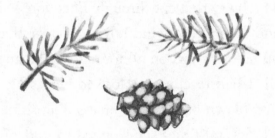

Chapter 34

Twigs Comes Clean

The young woolly had twisted around in alarm as if he'd gotten a snout full of something terribly familiar, something that he'd been telling himself he'd never smell again, something that connected him to home. Up ahead the buried trail ran beneath a large overpass that lifted a highway above it. If you were from ten thousand years ago and had never seen a road, much less a highway, you might have called the opening beneath that overpass a cave.

And there was a black, frothy swirl beneath the overpass that could have been mistaken for the mouth of a cave. It appeared to be some kind of whirlpool that had wind whipping around inside it, except that instead of pulling things in, it was spitting them out. Blades of grass and leaves off bushes and even some dark streams of smoke came spinning out.

For a second I wondered if I mightn't be playing dead and having myself yet another vision, but that didn't make sense. I hadn't heard any wind chimes. What's more, a branch blew by, grazing my head. I'd never before been beaned in a vision.

On either side of the whirlpool climbed two columns of lightning that didn't stop crackling as they reached upward into the dark, roiling clouds. I don't think I'd ever seen anything that so totally belonged in a movie. Inside the whirlpool it was blacker than a night sky stripped of everything that twinkles. Now and then a fork of lightning jigged around in there, showing a tunnel made of the most outstanding storm clouds imaginable. The tunnel stretched off into the distance as if it never came to an end.

"Can you see the vortex?" the 3000 asked.

"Dead ahead," I told her.

"You can drop me off here," Twigs said, sounding more afraid than me, if that's possible.

"Be honest," I called back to the galumpus. "Don't you want to go home just a little?"

"Not so's you'd notice," he sniffled loudly, to be heard above the wind. "I'm liking it here more and . . ." And here he broke down sobbing. "More."

"Twigs," I said, "is there something you're not telling us?"

"Not really," he waffled, sounding ready to bust apart at a seam and swamp us with his sorrows.

"Come on now," I coaxed. "You're with friends."

"Class," the 3000 said, "it is generally believed best . . . to talk about one's troubles."

That robot sounded awfully sure of herself, so I guess she had at least one subroutine still working. But our encouragements weren't enough to sway Twigs, which left me short-tempered as the mayor. With everything I'd put on the line here, it seemed as though that galumpus owed me a little something in return.

"Out with it!" I snapped. "What aren't you telling us?"

Yes, I felt a pang of regret for stooping to the mayor's level, but my outburst did get results. Everything that Twigs had been holding back came spilling out.

"You want to know the reason I can't go home?" the big galumpus cried. "I'll tell you the reason! I don't have a home to go back to. That's the reason."

For a second or two there the snow seemed to quit falling around us and start falling inside us, filling us with a silence so thick you'd leave footprints if you tried to walked through it.

"What are you talking about?" I pressed.

"There was a fire. Okay?"

The smoke spinning out of the time tunnel said yes to that. The catch in Twigs's voice made it sound as if he was to blame.

"How big a fire?" I asked.

"Big enough to burn up everything. That's why I can't go home. That home of mine—it's gone."

I didn't know what to say to that. It took a green robot from the future whose batteries were almost dead to handle a dilemma that thorny.

"Class," the 3000 said, "exactly how do you think the fire . . . started?"

Twigs hung his head and swayed his trunk back and forth in misery without end.

"How'd the fire start?" I nudged.

"I started it!" he blurted. "Okay? Me. I did it."

Ten thousand years ago I didn't think they had matches or cigarette lighters or electrical wires lying around, and so far as I knew, woolly mammoths didn't breathe fire. Something told me that only happened in movies about dragons. His story had some holes in it.

"How?" I asked.

"I just closed my eyes and did it. Okay? I was sick and tired of everyone treating me like I was nothing but a kid who didn't know anything. And my little sister could do no wrong. I was fed up with that, too. So I just closed my eyes and said it'd serve them right and wished them all away. And the next thing I knew there was smoke and they were gone. There were flames, too, and it was hot, awful hot, and I was running into that cave to get away from it all. Okay? Now do you understand why I can't go back?"

"Twigs," I said, "you can't start a fire that way."

"Oh yes you can," Twigs countered, not about to go easy on himself. "If you got a wisher like mine."

"No," I yelled to be heard above the whipping wind. "You can't start a fire by just thinking about it."

"I did."

"You're wrong," I loudly answered. "And I can prove it."

"How?"

"Try setting me on fire."

"No way!" Twigs cried out, astonished that I'd even suggest it. "Who'd put you out?"

"I would," the 3000 offered.

"Well, it don't matter," Twigs shouted. "I'm not mad enough at Gilly to set him on fire. He's been nice to me."

"Fair enough," the 3000 said. "So try to set me . . . on fire."

"Forget it," Twigs bawled. "I'm not mad enough at you either."

"What if I called you . . . a liar?" the 3000 crackled. "Would that help?"

"Say, now," Twigs squawked, "I'm no liar."

"Class," the 3000 asked, "what would you call some-one who . . . says they started a fire that they didn't start?"

"Now, just a minute," Twigs balked.

"Class?"

"You asked for it," Twigs warned.

The big galumpus squeezed shut his eyes and bunched up his brow until I thought his brains might pop. He grunted as if trying to uproot a tree. He sucked down a deep, deep breath and held it in as if his trunk were knotted.

Long as he went at it? I almost expected to see the 3000's green fur burst into flames. I really did. But almost doesn't count, not when it comes to starting fires. After a full minute, the 3000 wasn't the least bit smoky.

"See?" I yelled, trying to let Twigs down easy. "Whatever started that fire, it wasn't you."

"It was the cavemen," said the 3000.

"Huh?" yammered Twigs.

"They started the fire you're talking about," the 3000 explained, loud as she could manage. "I saw them.

319

The one with the wolf head had a . . . flint that he used. They wanted to separate you from your herd so they could collect your tusks. And they didn't burn down everything, only that meadow . . . by the lake."

"Are you sure?" Twigs asked.

I'd never heard anyone sound so relieved. Not even my cousin Frasier the day we told him it was all right to talk to himself, or my sister Selena when she passed her playing-dead test, or my niece Mulan when she found out she didn't have to act tough day and night—none of them sounded anywhere near as relieved as Twigs when he discovered he wasn't a firebug.

"My sensors definitely recorded it," the 3000 promised. "And your mother had the whole herd searching for you when you ran into . . . this time tunnel. You couldn't see them because of the smoke."

"What about Munch-Munch?" Twigs cried. "Is she okay?"

"The last I saw, she was fine too, a little scared was all."

"Then I need to get home," Twigs shouted, struggling to rise up on his gimpy leg.

"Class," the 3000 said, "I'm afraid we're not . . . ready for that. But almost."

"What's the holdup?" Twigs demanded.

"The cavemen. They need to go back too. But don't worry, they should be coming soon."

"Oh no they won't," Twigs corrected.

"Why not?" I called out.

"'Cause they're already here!"

Chapter 35

Now What?

The three cavemen staggered out of the blizzard with their heads bent against the wind. Boar-head held his fancy lampshade on with one hand and now had his golf bag slung over his shoulder with the other. Birdy's green mask remained atop a golf club, peeking over his shoulder. Wolf-head prodded Saber-tooth ahead like a prisoner. He'd retrieved his prize sunset picture and kept it tucked under an arm so that the wind couldn't grab it.

Saber-tooth was hunched up beneath his blue towel, hugging himself to keep warm. Tight as he pressed his toaster against his chest, he must have been expecting to be robbed any moment.

Same as ever, they jabbered at each other plenty rough until the 3000 raised her voice to interrupt them. Whatever she said to them, they didn't like it one bit and shouted back, shoving Saber-tooth forward as if that was their answer.

"Are they headed for the tunnel?" the 3000 asked me.

"No," I said, "they're headed toward us."

She may not have heard that. Her chin dipped as if she'd nodded off first. Her green fur lost its glow, going dark.

Seeing the 3000 fade that way made the cavemen all the friskier. As usual, they spread out to come at us from three different directions. Boar-head and Wolf-head took the flanks, leaving a shivering Saber-tooth sandwiched between them, where they could keep a close eye on him. Even so, Saber-tooth hung back a little, muttering to himself.

If that wasn't trouble enough, Twigs chose then to cry out, "Do I hear Ma?"

That sounded like wishful thinking to me. I couldn't hear anything but the wind whistling in my ears as if I was about to be blown clear into next summer.

"They're getting awfully close!" I yelled in the 3000's ear, for all the good it did.

She stayed dark, didn't answer. I might have panicked a little and punched her shoulder. It brought her back to life, halting the cavemen's advance.

"Class!" the 3000 weakly ordered. "Everyone . . . to the tunnel."

"Look out!" Twigs wailed.

Boar-head had dropped his golf bag and gotten close enough to club the 3000 over the head again. This time he completely flattened the 3000's round hat and knocked the black-eyed Susie loose.

The robot shivered.

Once.

Twice.

Her faint glow winked off awful permanent-like, though not before she managed to raise an arm and shoot one last feeble green ray from her palm. The burst lasted but a second and made Boar-head roar with laughter. Her aim was so off that it didn't go anywhere near him. But on second thought, I wasn't so sure she was trying to hit him. She might have been aiming for the mouth of the tunnel.

The green beam hit the time vortex dead center, flaring briefly. A deep boom rang out, as if something new had been set in motion. That was followed by a rumble that sounded like deer hooves clattering across a long wooden bridge. The pillars of lightning on either side of the tunnel flared brighter, crackling and sizzling, but only for an instant. Then they snuffed out. The wind whipping out the tunnel kicked up into a gale.

Without power the 3000 couldn't withstand the gusts and toppled sideways, forcing me to leap for the toboggan, where I landed with a belly-flop. *Ommmph!* While I was catching my breath, Wolf-head had a chance to spear me with his mop. He might have done it, too, if Twigs hadn't stepped in.

"Hey!" Twigs bellowed. "Pick on somebody your own size!"

The big galumpus swatted the caveman aside with his trunk, knocking loose the painting under his arm. The wind grabbed ahold of the sunset and sent it sailing. Wolf-head bellowed as if he'd just lost his shrunken root necklace. The old caveman turned on us with fire in his eyes and fire in his belly and maybe some flames between his toes, too.

And then came more troubles.

The wind died away to nothing and it got dreadful chilly and still. The snow fell straight down.

The stillness dragged on long enough for the cavemen to regroup. Pulling Saber-tooth aside, they ripped the toaster out of his arms and tossed it away. His father straightened him up, whipped the blue towel off his shoulders, and flung it aside. That done, he roared into Saber-tooth's ear. Wolf-head got going on the boy's other ear.

"I think this might be the end," Twigs said, facing the spear pointed our way.

"It's possible," I agreed.

"It ain't right," Twigs groaned. "I'll never get a

chance to tell my ma and pa and sis, and the rest of the herd, that I didn't mean all those terrible things I said."

"Tell them now," I said.

"What good will that do? They won't hear me."

"Maybe that's not what's counts."

"Well, what is?"

"That you wanted to tell them," I said.

"Are you sure about that?"

"Hardly," I admitted. "But what other choice do you have?" And then, to prove my point, I raised my voice and shouted at the top of my lungs. I let loose with something that I'd been saving up for a long spell: "Mayor Crawdaddy, you're an old fuddy-duddy!"

Maybe I was onto something. That felt grand.

"A-gosh," Twigs said. "Do you think he heard you?"

"I hope so." Raising my voice again, I added, "You too, Sussex. Fuddy-duddy!" Then back to Twigs: "There. Much better. You try it."

And Twigs did.

The big galumpus tilted back his head and trumpeted for all he was worth. My hackles rose to hear it.

Such a long, wavery note . . . I don't think Theodore Wirth Park had heard anything so fine for at least ten thousand years. The trumpet of Ruth's brother couldn't begin to compare. If there was a scrap of justice anywhere, I had to believe that his ma and pa and sis and herd had gotten the message too.

"Now what?" Twigs asked.

"We fight," I said, hoping that wasn't wind chimes I was hearing in the background. It would have been an awfully embarrassing time to black out.

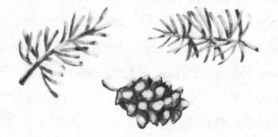

Chapter 36

Them Again?

Twigs turned into a different woolly mammoth once he found out he hadn't burned his home down. The whimpering, the whining—all gone. He swatted with his trunk, flashed his tusks, and ordered the 3000 to rise and shine.

"Come on!" Twigs bellowed. "It's time to go!"

No answer from the 3000, though.

Boar-head and Wolf-head screamed at Saber-tooth to get closer. How do I know that's what they were saying? The way they shoved him forward whenever he tried to back off. Also, the young caveman threatened them with his spear. His cheeks were puffing, his arms trembling. For a second, I thought he might try to run them through, but in the end, Boar-head cowed him into coming at us again.

Twigs struggled to his feet only to collapse back on his rump. That twisted leg of his may have kept him down, but it didn't dampen his spirits. He trumpeted at those cavemen until they held up—briefly. I sat back-to-back with him on the toboggan, proud to make a last stand with him, hissing and spitting for all I was worth, just like in the movies.

I knew we were in serious trouble when Boar-head started talking to us as if we were old pals. Wolf-head was cackling and bobbing his head agreeably, too, as if our end was near. But what tipped me off more than anything? The way Saber-tooth was glowering at us as if his troubles were all our fault.

Often as not when things seem the darkest, it turns out that I'm wrong. As Mayor Crawdaddy is fond of reminding me—*Gilly, there's always plenty of time for it to get darker.* Floodwaters can always rise higher. How many times had the last little scrap of hope I'd been clinging to had been snatched away by even worse events? And I appeared headed down that same twisty, dark path again.

Unannounced, a beat-up car with smashed headlights came scraping and grinding through the storm as if ready to give those caveman a hand. The sunset picture stuck to its crumpled front bumper had Wolf-head doing a gleeful jig. I braced myself for the worst, wondering what next. Peering closer, I saw that someone sitting on the car's front seat was screaming at us—that's what.

But wait . . .

It was Ruth! She was scrunched forward behind the cracked windshield, trying to see past the bent wiper blades that were whapping back and forth. She'd managed to convince her brother to try to rescue us. Birdy had probably helped, keen as he'd been to see a rip in the fabric of the space-time continuum.

"Them again?" Twigs croaked, not sure if he should be relieved or worried. "Don't they know I've got to get home?"

The car wheezed to a stop. Steam hissed out from beneath its hood. Ruth's brother leaned out the driver's window and blew his trumpet. Birdy shook his light sword out a rear window. Ruth was slapping the dash and shouting something that sounded like a warning, although without the 3000's help, we had no idea what she was saying. For all we knew, she could have been asking for directions to the time tunnel, which was hard to see now that the wind and pillars of lightning were gone.

The cavemen looked as lost as us about what she was yelling. They shook their club and mop at her, and did some hollering of their own. Or at least that's what Boar-head and Wolf-head did. Saber-tooth, he'd slipped off to the side, acting sort of relieved.

"Gilly!" Ruth cried, waving me toward the car.

I waved back, motioning her toward us. If they really wanted to help, I told her, they could tow the toboggan over to the time vortex before the tunnel completely fell apart. I could have made a whole lot of other suggestions, too, for all the good it would have done. She still couldn't understand me any better than I could understand her.

"Gilly!" she repeated.

Now, did she really think we could get Twigs inside that car? Especially with his bum leg? And to reach the car we had to get past the cavemen, didn't we? How were we supposed to manage that? They weren't looking any too cooperative at the moment. No, Ruth wasn't thinking straight, if that was her plan. But no matter. Her heart was in the right place. And I know I'll never get tired of remembering what she came up with next. It was the best worst idea I'd ever met, and by far the most helpful.

When Twigs and I didn't budge, Ruth threw open her door, wrenched the trumpet away from her brother's lips, and tried coming to us. I do believe she planned to give the trumpet to the cavemen if they'd let Twigs go. Talk about brilliant. The way those cavemen prized that horn, they just might have gone for it.

She never made it out of the car though. Her brother

snagged her first. A scuffle broke out. There was plenty of shouting to go with it. In the end, the brother won, wrestling back his trumpet.

That didn't stop Ruth, though. Now she snatched her brother's hat, the one with the woolly earflaps that looked so warm, and scooted for her door again. She might have been hoping to swap the hat for Twigs, but Birdy put a stop to that.

While Ruth and her brother had been struggling, Birdy had climbed out of the car's back seat. With a swish of his bathrobe, he'd positioned himself before the cavemen. His light sword was drawn for one last stand. He looked flat-out heroic until the green light of his sword fizzled and died.

It didn't matter, though.

Seeing Ruth rebel against her older brother had opened Saber-tooth's eyes to new horizons. Liking what he saw, he turned on Boar-head and Wolf-head to unload some screams of his own. It sounded as though he was uncorking grudges that had been bottled up inside him for ages. His outburst dumbfounded the older cavemen. They acted as if someone had slapped brand-new eyes in their heads, as if they'd never really seen Saber-tooth before. Whatever he said felt so good that he screamed it all over again.

I can't be sure, but I might have just witnessed the start of a new human development—teenage rebellion. If Saber-tooth managed to carry his attitude ten thousand years into the past, it could have been growing in popularity ever since, explaining some family scenes I'd witnessed in the park.

And Saber-tooth wasn't done, either. Now that he had his pa's full, undivided attention, he needed an encore, something that would drive home his point that they couldn't boss him around, that he wasn't a kid anymore. And after a moment the perfect solution came to him. Taking two steps, he planted his feet and hurled his spear into the blizzard with all his might.

Time got all muddled and slow.

The spear took forever and a day to leave his hand, and all the while it was taking off, Boar-head and Wolf-head looked stunned as pollywogs in sunlight.

Boar-head's club dropped to his side. Wolf-head let go of his mop as if its handle had scorched him. There was a serious chance that both their mouths might never close again.

With everyone watching, the spear climbed higher and higher until it disappeared into the falling snow. For all I know, it's still climbing to this day, headed for the moon or nearest star or a galaxy where there's purple rain.

Saber-tooth smiled the whole while. Even the Earl of Sussex had never looked prouder than that boy, which was saying something. The red squirrel could barely scratch under his arm without acting as if he'd performed a miracle.

Of course, time didn't stand still while all that was going on. Some movement off to the side caught my eye. The wind was picking up again.

At first it was barely a slight breeze, swirling the falling snow. But there was one tiny difference—its direction. The wind wasn't blowing out of the tunnel anymore. Now the time tunnel was slowly but surely sucking air into it.

And speaking of the tunnel, the rumbling inside it had returned, far away but drumming closer.

I sure would have liked to puzzle over what all that meant. It would have beat all to pieces doing what I had to, which was help protect us from Boar-head and Wolf-head. The two of them were acting madder than stepped-on sow bugs. They may have written Saber-tooth off as a lost cause, but that didn't mean they'd forgotten about us. No, they seemed keener than ever to salvage something from their outing. Boar-head grabbed his club, and Wolf-head took up his mop and pried his sunset painting off the car's front bumper. They both stomped our way as if on a mission.

Well, Ruth started honking the car's horn, and her brother trumpeted, and Birdy yelled threats, and the wind kept on picking up, but none of that was enough to slow those two cavemen down, not a bit.

Saber-tooth tried screaming at them.

I let them have it too.

Twigs trumpeted.

None of it did a speck of good. They were determined to finish what they'd started out to do—collect Twigs's tusks.

In the end, it took something else entirely to stop

them from lowering the boom on us, and that's why the extra time that Ruth's and Saber-tooth's rebellion had bought us became so important.

The rumbling from inside the time vortex kept on doubling every second. A brownish blur came bursting out of the tunnel, and it wasn't any herd of mice that showed up. A stampeding herd of woolly mammoths thundered straight our way. The lead one had a huge pair of curved tusks that looked sturdy enough to rip a hole in the space-time continuum all on their own. Those cavemen scattered like pigeons before a fire truck.

"Ma!" cried Twigs.

Chapter 37

The Dragon Creek Herd

As soon as Twigs's ma saw that his leg was hurt, she grabbed ahold of the toboggan's rope with her trunk and pulled him back toward the tunnel. I got pitched off the sled as it jolted forward but did manage to shout, "Take the 3000!" I didn't figure that green bear wanted to be left behind in our time.

"They saved me," Twigs called out.

One of the mammoths curled her trunk around the 3000 and carried her off.

"What about that furry little thing?" asked another mammoth.

"Him too," Twigs answered, meaning that I'd also helped save him.

But in all the hubbub, that woolly must have figured that Twigs meant she should grab me. That's how I got plucked out of a snowdrift and carted along. No amount of protesting got me dropped, either. There's wasn't a whole lot of listening going on just then.

So the herd stampeded back into the vortex, which sucked us all ahead. Talk about deafening. Fifteen to twenty woolly mammoths pulling a toboggan while running full tilt was louder than a passing coal train.

Behind us the older cavemen were raging and jumping up and down and threatening the terriblest kind of smashing and bashing and gnashing if they ever got their hands on us. But that was all for show. They didn't come anywhere close to rushing after us. Saber-tooth stood off to the side, looking sort of pleased, as if he'd put in the best day's work of his life.

Birdy gave me a smart salute, but Ruth saw my predicament and tried scrambling out of the car to rescue

341

me. Her brother grabbed the back of her coat to stop her. And then Theodore Wirth Park disappeared behind me . . .

That tunnel had some length. With the wind at our back, we hurled forward faster than swifts. The roar in my ears never let up. Everything was the deepest, thickest, most gunked-up kind of black except when lightning flickered off on the edges. Then for a split second everything got blindingly bright and the air tingled and Twigs forgot he was almost five and squealed. I cut loose a few choice words for Mayor Crawdaddy and the Earl of Sussex, and this time I went considerably beyond calling them fuddy-duddies.

Finally, a smudge of dirty light showed up way ahead of us. I wouldn't exactly call it daylight, but it leaned that way, growing wider and nearer and less dingy until without warning, the tunnel quit and we all tumbled out its other end. We crashed onto a knoll that overlooked a meadow of wavering grass. Small islands of stunted timber dotted the land. Up above, the sky was stuffed full of dark thunderheads that banged around without shedding a drop of rain. It was summer. It was hot. The snowflakes blown out of the tunnel with us turned to mist before hitting the ground. Right away a swarm of oversized bugs got all lovey-dovey. In the distance the tongues of grass fires tried to lick the threatening sky.

To avoid getting trampled by the herd pouring out of the tunnel behind us, we had to hustle out of the way. Even so there was a large pile-up of woolly mammoths as some in front lost their footing and fell. A good deal of bugling and trumpeting followed as those woolly mammoths called each other names.

"Moss-tusk!"

"Plugged-trunk!"

"Twinkle-toes!"

Twigs's mother didn't waste any time taking him to task.

"I thought I told you to never wander off," she unloaded.

"It won't happen again," Twigs promised.

"It better not. And what happened to your leg?"

The way Twigs went on about being stepped on by a speeding beast with burning eyes? And nearly chewed to bits by a beast with churning teeth? And screamed at by a beast who was louder than thunder? He made it sound as though you couldn't turn around in Theodore Wirth without taking your life in your hands. The Earl of Sussex couldn't have made the place sound half as dangerous.

Stern as his ma studied him? I'm pretty sure all that saved him from a world-class lecture about fibbing was the strange gurgling, slurping sounds coming from the vortex. The time tunnel was swaying from side to side as if a giant was shaking it by the tail. Then its mouth started to shrink. Air blasted out of it with a hiss. Just before closing completely shut, it spit out the three cavemen as if they tasted bad.

The three of them rolled across the grass, broken and bruised and battered. Their animal skins were crooked and torn. Boar-head's lampshade and golf bag went flying. Wolf-head totally lost his grip on his mop, and his sunset painting went cartwheeling away. Saber-tooth had reclaimed his toaster and managed to hold on to it when he landed, but not for long. Boar-head tore it away from him and flung it into the tall grass.

And that was just the start of the show.

Saber-tooth got a real dressing-down for all the trouble and disappointment he'd caused. No longer freezing beneath iced-up skins, the boy sassed back. That heated up Boar-head and Wolf-head hotter than ever. Their shouting lasted until they noticed they weren't alone. A lineup of woolly mammoths towered above them, watching their every move.

The herd didn't say a word. They didn't have to. The cavemen took the hint and made themselves scarce, scrambling off into the tall grass as if their lives depended on it, which they probably did. Saber-tooth tried snagging his toaster on the way, but Boar-head wasn't having any of that and hauled him away over his protests. Tall grass muffled the last of what they said.

As for the Smokey 3000, she never did come around. The woolly mammoth who was carrying her unfurled his trunk, which sent her rolling across the ground until she bumped against the toboggan and lay still.

"Smokey?" I pleaded, nudging her shoulder. "What am I supposed to do now?"

It was Twigs who answered from the back of the toboggan: "You can live with us."

"We're very, very grateful," Twigs's mother assured me after hearing her son go on about all we'd done for him.

I bowed and told them that on behalf of Theodore Wirth Park I was glad to be of service. The mayor would have blathered on lots longer, making everyone feel a hundred times more beholden. He'd have dressed it all up with a lot of humbug, too, as was his style. But anyway, the mammoths seemed satisfied enough with what I'd said.

"I do kind of have one little question though," I said. "Do you have any idea on how I might go about getting home?"

The time vortex had completely vanished by then with a pipsqueak of a pop, and I didn't know how to call it back.

"No, really," Twigs insisted, "you can live with us forever."

His ma wasn't terribly excited about that extended invitation, but she recovered nicely, saying, "Why, yes. We wouldn't have it any other way."

And that's how I became an honorary member of the Dragonfly Creek herd, the only possum ever granted the honor. The mayor would have been eaten alive with envy and jealousy and longing if he'd seen me riding around on Twigs's shoulders like some kind of bigshot. The Earl of Sussex would have been thrown into an everlasting snit.

How they would have felt about being stranded ten thousand years in the past was another matter. I know it left me feeling all broken up and empty as a crumpled pop can to think about how far from home I'd landed.

If I ever hear anyone holding forth on what makes a place home, I'll make sure they add *time* to the list. Here I was, standing on the same patch of land that would someday become Theodore Wirth Park, but it wasn't anything like home at all. It felt about as far away from home as I could get. And there I stood, lost right where I'd been living all my life, just ten thousand years too early. I was getting an awfully big dose of how Twigs must have felt when he'd found himself in our time—snuffly, discombobulated, and full of yearnings I couldn't slap a name on.

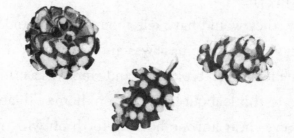

Chapter 38

The Christopher 100

Weeks paraded past. Summer's thunderstorms dwindled, which only made the fires spread. It wasn't a stretch to see why Twigs imagined he'd started a blaze. Some days you could barely see the sun through the haze and smoke, and what sun you could see looked ghostly. Whole stands of timber went up in flames, huge patches of grass were nothing but soot.

While his leg healed, Twigs rode the toboggan

behind his mother, who didn't know what to make of me. Possums didn't live in the area ten thousand years ago, or at least not that I could find any traces of. When I asked if they'd ever noticed any possums in the neighborhood, the mammoths chewed on twigs and grass real thoughtful-like before saying, "Nope."

"You're a funny little thing," Twigs's mother said when I tried to describe what Theodore Wirth Park was like in my time, with city and roads and lights surrounding it.

"Ma," Twigs said, embarrassed, "where Gilly lives there's people all over the place. I saw them."

"If you say so, dear," she answered, dismissing what he'd said with a wag of her trunk.

"Geez," Twigs later apologized to me. "She just doesn't get it."

Eventually Twigs's leg mended well enough for him to climb off the toboggan and gimp around on his own. For the rest of his life he'd limp, but he got around well enough for the herd to start talking about moving on to better grass. At least, they claimed it would be better. I wouldn't know, never having developed a taste for the stuff. Twigs was awful keen for me to join them, but I begged off, saying I better stick around the 3000.

"What if she comes back to life?" I said. "She won't know where she is, and she'll be all alone."

"I don't know." Twigs sized up the 3000. "She don't look so good."

"But she's my only shot at getting home."

Or at least that's the explanation I gave for not traveling on with the herd, though there were other reasons. I hate to complain, but woolly mammoths aren't big talkers. They were usually too busy chewing on things to bother with it, and when they did get around to saying something, it wasn't about anything I found too interesting.

"That blue-stemmed grass is kind of tasty."

"If you don't mind chewing on it till your eyes cross."

So even though I was surrounded by a whole herd, it got kind of lonely.

But don't go thinking that was the only reason I passed on joining them. There were others. I couldn't ride on Twigs's shoulder every hour of every day. I had to get down to forage for grubs and roots and such if I wanted to eat anything tasty. And when I did get down, the rest of the herd wasn't all that careful about where they stepped. Twigs nagged and pleaded with them to watch where they were going, but that didn't save my tail from getting trampled.

And then there was Twigs's little sister Munch-Munch, who wasn't so little and became a big problem. She was jealous that her brother had a possum for a friend and wanted one herself. Thank goodness Twigs wasn't willing to share.

That threw his sister into a real tizzy. She tried making a mud possum to carry around on her back, but it didn't look enough like me to give satisfaction. She pestered her ma to make Twigs share me, but their mother said no, she wasn't old enough to hang around with a possum. I might put funny ideas into her head. His sister finally decided to make me go away on her own. First she tried wishing me away, but she wasn't any better at wishing than her brother was. Next, she gave sitting on me a whirl. Big as she was, that certainly would have worked if I hadn't been too quick for her. Still, I had to be on high alert day and night with her around. It gave me a strong inkling about why Twigs had wanted to get away from everyone.

The last thing Twigs ever said to me?

"I'll wish you home."

He made that promise over his shoulder while his mother prodded him after the rest of the herd. The call of fresh grass lured them onward.

"Take care of yourself," I yelled after him, adding in a smaller, fond voice, "You big galumpus."

As for Twigs wishing me home—nope. He needed more practice before making something like that happen. I stayed right where I was, watching the Dragonfly Creek herd get smaller in the distance.

Gathering together the lampshade, golf bag, mop, sunset painting, and toaster, I piled them near the toboggan and made camp near the 3000. Pulling the clubs out of the golf bag made it into a cozy den. I set Birdy's green mask atop the bag, hoping to scare off uninvited guests, and to give me a little company.

Once in a great while I could have sworn that the

3000 whirred or clicked or had a hair tip that glowed ever so briefly. Wishful thinking? Possibly. But it sure seemed as though there might be a tiny, restless spark roving about inside that bear.

Weeks flickered past.

Frost danced in the morning light. Winter prowled nearby. The nights got powerfully crisp. Ten thousand years ago, the night sky didn't have room for a single more star.

I never did see the cavemen again, though I often wondered about Saber-tooth, how he was getting along with his pa after standing up for himself.

But mostly it was just me and the 3000, two specks marooned in the far distant past. I was at least a hundred different shades of homesick. And Birdy's mask wasn't satisfying company. Whenever I got really blue and lonesome and pining something terrible to see another possum, I gazed at myself in the toaster's chrome side. My reflection never answered any of the questions I asked, but at least it kept a little kernel of hope alive inside me. I daydreamed about how grand my homecoming would be if I got back to Theodore Wirth. I even told myself that if I ever made it home I'd do my best to let bygones be bygones with the mayor and Sussex.

At such times, the only thing that helped fill the hollow spot deep inside me was gazing up at the moon. It cast a blue-white light that made the air shine as if scrubbed and brought to mind the welcoming glow of Ruth's TV ten thousand years from now. Thinking of her someday wearing a veterinarian's coat always brought on a smile.

Then late in the fall, a pack of wolves discovered my camp. One moment the 3000 and I were all alone. The next a circle of great gray brutes appeared. They rested on their haunches, examining us as if they'd never seen a bear in a park ranger's uniform or a possum peeking out of a golf bag. They paid particular attention to the green mask.

That didn't last long, though.

Once they figured out the mask couldn't do anything but look at them, they pounced. Gleaming teeth lunged from everywhere. A chorus of snarling and snapping drowned out any squeals someone might have been making.

Woodsmoke and wind chimes overcame me, but not before I glimpsed the 3000 being tossed in the air and tugged on from several directions and smashed against a nearby boulder.

And then I was riding on my mother's back with all my brothers and sisters.

Sometime later, when I slowly came to, I found myself still in one piece. So was the 3000. The wolf pack hadn't managed to take a single bite out of that green bear or rip loose a thread of her uniform. Whoever had put the 3000 together had made her wolf-proof.

All of the banging and slamming had brought about one small change, though. A dinky red bulb had popped out of the tip of the 3000's nose. That was new. And as I groggily watched, it flashed, or at least I hoped it had.

That brought me around in a hurry. I had to wait a while before it flashed again, but eventually it did. I hadn't been imaging things. It kept on flashing too. Several times a day. It seemed as if the 3000 was trying to speak to me. After that, life was a dab less lonely.

A week later, while rooting around Dragonfly Creek, I heard a crash and hurried back to camp, not knowing what to expect. I was awfully right about that.

A silver boy wearing the same brown park ranger uniform as the 3000 had tried lifting the green bear to her feet, though she hadn't stayed upright for long. She'd crumpled to the ground by the time I reached them, and the boy was opening a small door on the back of her neck. I'd never noticed that door before. The boy was poking at something inside it.

"Who are you?" I asked, kind of astonished and squeaky-like.

Turning my way, he answered, "A Christopher 100."

"What are you doing to Smokey?"

"Trying to reboot her, without success. It looks as though I'm going to have to take her into the shop for total diagnostics."

"Does that mean you're from the future?"

He didn't answer me right away. Instead, he stood there studying me with the sun glinting off his high silver forehead. The cloud of gnats surrounding him didn't bother him at all. A little antenna popped out the top of his park ranger hat and swiveled around as if waiting to receive instructions.

"Who are you?" the silver boy asked

"Gilly," I said. "I was helping this Smokey 3000 because a temporal displacement incident threw her into my time, which is about ten thousand years ahead of now. Any chance you could get me back there?"

After looking over the toboggan and golf bag and all the other stuff in my camp, he said, "Silly old possum, I think I'd better. To protect against time contamination." It appeared I'd found my ticket home.

"How'd you find us?" I asked.

"This unit's distress beacon went off," he said, pointing at the red bulb on the 3000's snout.

So the 3000 had saved me after all, with a little help from that wolf pack. It turned out that the Christopher 100 worked with the 3000 in the Theodore Wirth Wildlife and Time Preservation Sanctuary, and that they'd been searching for her whereabouts since the electrical storm had scrambled her circuits. After he'd gathered me, the 3000, and everything else that the cavemen had dragged back from my time, something deep inside him started humming.

"Give me a moment," the Christopher 100 said. Flipping open the tip of his pinkie, he pulled out a wire that he threaded inside the little door on the 3000's neck. "I've got to access her time log to find out exactly

when you're from." He concentrated briefly before saying, "Got it. Hold on!"

I did.

The parkland of prairie grass and evergreens of ten thousand years ago began to fade from view.

The next thing I knew we were standing in a familiar blizzard. Sheltering us was an overpass that I'd seen before, though this time there wasn't a tunnel swirling beneath it.

"The less said about your adventure, the better," the silver boy advised.

"Why's that?"

"Time contamination," he explained. "Also, who'd believe you?"

With that he tucked the Smokey 3000 over his shoulder and started to hum again. He must have been way stronger than he looked, 'cause he was half the 3000's size yet handled her with ease. A moment later he vanished into the snowstorm as if he'd never been there. I knew that wasn't true. It couldn't be. If he'd never been there, then how had all the stuff from my campsite ended up stacked beside me? And where had the 3000 gone to?

To keep their faint outline from disappearing completely, I did my best not to blink. But in the end—I blinked. Opening my eyes, I found them gone, back to the future, which no longer seemed as far away as it once had. After what I'd been through, the future seemed way closer than ever before, as if I could reach out and touch tomorrow, same as yesterday had touched me.

Chapter 39

A Funeral

Two nights later the blizzard finally piddled out, and I left the snow cave where I'd holed up, leaving behind everything that had traveled with me into the distant past. Come the spring thaw, the abandoned golf bag and clubs, mop, toboggan, toaster, sunset painting, and green mask would leave some park employees scratching their heads. I hoped they'd get it all back to the rightful owners.

The moon made the snowfields around me as

silver and lovely as an old black-and-white movie. Half-starved, I headed for Ruth's, dreaming of crunchy peanut butter. The quickest way there was straight through the quaking bog, where I met up with a gathering of park animals solemnly gazing into the pond's dark water. Mayor Crawdaddy was addressing them.

"He was as noble and loyal and trustworthy a friend as any of us will ever know in this vale of tears." The mayor had rolled out his best silken voice to deliver that, the one that never failed to leave you feeling goose-bumpy to the core. "There can't be any doubt that he was brave to the very end."

"And beyond," the Earl of Sussex chipped in, pressing a paw over his heart.

At first I didn't pick up on who they were going on about. All I could tell was that every animal in the park had shined up their whiskers and tailfeathers for the occasion. Flocks of birds filled the tamarack branches, looking down on the proceedings. Gigi had marched all her grandkids out of their dens to pay their last respects. The storm must have claimed someone important. Why, every possum I knew had shown up, and as a general rule, we tend to be awfully superstitious about attending funerals.

"'Cause if there's one thing we all know," the mayor went on, his tone daring anyone to say otherwise, "it's that this park won't ever be the same without him."

Everyone got all choked up thinking about soldiering on without whoever we'd lost. They were blowing their noses and wiping their eyes and bowing their heads. Wanting to hear who we were sending off, I pulled up behind a tamarack without announcing my return. I was planning to hang around just long enough to hear a name, then push on to Ruth's for some grub.

"It's a sad, sad day," Sussex heaped on, doing his best to keep up with the mayor.

"Oh that it weren't so," Crawdaddy lamented. "And I want you all to know that we did everything in our power to save that brave soul from such a bitter end, but he wouldn't have it. Said he didn't want anyone else risking it. Now, doesn't that have his name written all over it?"

"Yes, indeed," Sussex sighed. "Yes, indeed."

"It just goes to show that when your time has come,

even friendship and courage and resolve can't keep the seasons from turning."

Crawdaddy was in rare form all right, just pouring it on without shame. His voice had a velvety depth to it that plucked every heartstring within reach.

"Too true," Sussex added. "Too true."

"It's somehow fitting that we're all gathered here on the very bog he loved so dear. The very place he showed us all his finest hour." The mayor paused to collect himself and give the crowd a chance to wipe their eyes. After the sniffles dried up, he carried on, "And I do believe we should all take solace in the knowledge that in the end he sacrificed himself so that a poor child who'd been lost for ten thousand years could be reunited with his mother."

Wait a minute . . .

"Goodbye, Gilly," Sussex blubbered as if we'd been blood brothers. "You weren't nothing but the best."

The frauds! They were burying me with full honors, as if there'd never been a cross word between us, as if they'd been right beside me to the end, when Twigs had really needed their help. I almost stormed up front to say *NOT SO FAST!* But just then my empty stomach grumbled as if about to rip itself in half, and thinking about a handout from Ruth, I put on the brakes. And all right, maybe I was a teensy bit curious to hear the rest of my sendoff.

"His name will be forever remembered," the mayor sailed on. "So long as there's someone who still honors heroic deeds and true-blue character and unselfish gifts."

"He had 'em all," Sussex testified.

Right about then everybody broke down sobbing in the most helpless way, even the bucks and wild turkeys who normally don't shed a tear for anything. The woods rang with their snorts and gobbles. I saw the mayor pass Sussex a sign, as if to say, *Not a peep! Let 'em weep.* I hate to say it, but it was a tiny bit gratifying to hear how much I was going to be missed. It's not every day you get a chance to attend your own funeral, not even if you're a possum. I'd go so far as to almost recommend it if you're feeling blue or underappreciated. It can certainly perk you up. So I kind of settled in behind a tamarack tree to catch a little more about how remarkable I'd been. It wasn't bitter medicine to swallow.

"I wish now," the mayor confessed, all blue and achy, "that I'd told him more often how much I appreciated all the little things he did for me and everyone else in the park."

"Me too," Sussex blubbered. "Me too."

I wish they'd told me that just once.

"And I'm downright sorry about the time or two I might have mistakenly taken credit for some good deed that he'd done."

"I know that's true," Sussex said, earning a sharp look from the mayor.

"And if I ever cross paths with him in the Great Beyond," the mayor shoved on, "I'm for sure going to beg his forgiveness."

"As will I," Sussex echoed. "As will I."

That sealed it. I wasn't about to pass up an opportunity as golden as that. Seeing the mayor beg in public? I guessed my stomach could gurgle a little longer.

"I'm mighty glad to hear it," I called out, stepping out of hiding.

There was a gasp that came close to knocking over trees. It was followed by a power of silence. A dropped pine needle would have been deafening right about then. The mayor nearly fell over backward with a paw clamped over his chest. That was satisfying. Sussex cleared out as if he'd seen a ghost. That was even more satisfying.

Everyone parted to let me through. A few reached out to touch me kind of timid-like as I passed by. Just to make sure it was me. A three-legged mutt who'd been scooped up by a dogcatcher couldn't have wished for a better homecoming.

Once next to the mayor, I turned to face all my friends and neighbors and relatives. After a minute or two of soaking up everyone's astonishment, I told them what they were dying to hear.

"I got that big galumpus back to his own time," I reported. "And he asked me to thank all of you for your help and support."

That went over pretty well. For a moment everybody basked in the glow of the good deed we'd done for that poor lost woolly. Then they all crowded forward to pat me on the back, and ask for details, and say that they'd suspicioned all along that if anybody could get that galumpus home, it would be me.

As you might guess, none of that went down too smooth with Mayor Crawdaddy, who'd been shunted off to the side as everyone pressed around me. Oh, he acted glad enough to see me and clucked about what a relief it was to have me back home in one piece, but he couldn't stomach playing second fiddle forever. Putting up with it for even a minute or two was a strain.

"Say, Gilly," he piped up after a bit, "whatever happened to that green bear? Was she of any help at all?"

I knew right where he was going with that. He was inching his way toward letting everyone know that I hadn't exactly done everything by myself. All fine and good. I didn't plan on hogging the limelight forever, but before I got around to giving the 3000 her due, I couldn't resist posing one little question of my own.

"Do you mean before or after you and Sussex got scared and bailed out?"

That hit the mayor where he lived, and he blustered defensively, "Is that what you thought happened?"

Good thing that Gigi was there. The woodchuck called him on it right away.

"Oh, I think we all know how you and Earl operate," Gigi scolded. "That lost galumpus was just plain lucky to have Gilly by his side."

After that everyone crowded even closer to me and fawned over me in the most outrageous and satisfying way, saying they'd be honored if I'd join them for dinner. Some wondered if they could name their firstborn after me. One or two even went so far as to suggest that maybe I ought to consider running for mayor myself, seeing as how I already appeared to be doing most of the work.

Without sharing any goodbyes, Mayor Crawdaddy slunk off to lick his wounds. As catastrophes went, this one couldn't have turned out better.

And then, just when everything seemed about as perfect as it could get, a faint trumpeting came sliding through the woods. It sounded as if Twigs was bidding us farewell from ten thousand years back. Everyone lifted their head in earnest appreciation. Secret smiles blossomed on faces as we all remembered the lost galumpus.

Of course, it may have only been Ruth's brother fooling around with that horn of his in the moonlight, but I wasn't about to mention the possibility. I didn't want to wreck a moment so sweet as that.

Thinking of Ruth's brother reminded me of where I'd been headed before I got sidetracked by my funeral. That started my stomach to gurgling and growling livelier than ever. So I took my leave, telling everyone that I needed to go thank the girl who'd helped get that young galumpus home.

And that's what I did, headed straight for the glow of Ruth's bedroom. Happy to see me, she nearly fell out of her window giving me a hug. The two of us chattered back and forth as if we could understand each other perfectly. Maybe on some deep level we could. I say that because after a while she hunted up a dinner roll for me, one that she'd slathered with peanut butter, the crunchy kind. One taste of that told me for sure that I was home.

Chapter 40

One Last Word

Not too long after that, I finally had my fill of Mayor Crawdaddy and gave my resignation.

"What?" the Earl of Sussex quipped. "Too good to work with us?"

The mayor and Earl hadn't taken kindly to my celebrityhood.

"No, I've had a better job offer."

"Are you sure about that?" the mayor huffed. "Once you're gone, there won't be any coming back, you know."

He was convinced I had my eye on his job. Elections were coming up.

I suppose I should have told him not to worry, that after all that had happened, the last thing I wanted to be was mayor. But I held back. For one thing, he wouldn't have believed me. For another, there had been some unflattering stories circulating about me since my return from the dead. I'm talking about stories that suggested maybe things weren't nearly as rosy for Twigs as I'd painted them. After all, there weren't any woolly mammoths roaming around Theodore Wirth these days, were there? So what had happened to them? They were awfully big critters to just vanish. Somehow the stories making the rounds managed to suggest that I might have had something to do with their extinction.

I didn't wear myself out wondering where such stories as that might have come from. No doubt the mayor and Sussex were behind them. Who else? That's why I left them dangling about what my future plans might be.

A night later I started my new job. As arranged, I took myself to a far corner of the park, away from prying eyes. Actually, the spot was close to the overpass where the time tunnel had been. There I waited in a walnut tree for my ride to show up.

Eventually a soft whir filled the night air. My ears perked up. Out of nowhere a glowing green bear dressed in a park ranger's uniform appeared.

"Are you ready?" The 3000 sounded back to normal.

"Crunchy peanut butter?" I asked, wanting to be sure.

"As promised."

"Then I'm ready."

"Put this on," the 3000 said, handing me a small name tag.

"What's it say?"

"Opossum."

It stuck to my side like tape. With that in place, the 3000 lifted me off the low branch where I'd been waiting, and started to hum. Gradually the park began to disappear around us, replaced by a large room with rows and rows of young students. We materialized on a raised stage in front of them. An excited hush swept through the room as the haze swirling around us vanished.

The silver boy known as the Christopher 100 was

already talking to the audience. Introducing us, I guess. Naturally I couldn't understand what he was telling them, but when he was done, a girl raised her hand. The silver boy pointed at her, and she stood, asking what must have been a question. The Christopher 100 translated it for me.

"She wants to know if you have a favorite postage stamp."

Answering that triggered a flurry of other questions that kept the Christopher 100's translation program hopping. Straightening out their misunderstandings about my time took a while. First I had to let them know that animals in the park didn't use postage stamps because we couldn't read. Gasps. Or write. More gasps. So we had no reason to send letters by mail, which was what postage stamps were used for.

"Are you sure?" the girl asked, and the Christopher 100 translated.

And that was just the start of their questions about my time. Something told me that a few of them hadn't been paying as close attention to their studies as they might have.

"Do you know any dinosaurs?"

"Are acorns really trees?"

"What about seashells?"

"Tell us about cars!"

"Have you ever been to the moon?"

"Or Mars?"

"Do you know any knock-knock jokes?"

"How many flowers have you smelled?"

And more.

Once I'd answer all their questions, the Smokey 3000 led everyone outside for a field trip through the park. I demonstrated how to find and follow a trail, dig for grubs, and climb a tree. A yellow cat with a name tag that said *Cat* showed up. We hissed at each other. My grand climax was playing dead when a dog ambushed me. He had a name tag, too. *Dog.* Coming back to life earned me a big round of applause. Everybody wanted me to do it again.

After that, one lucky kid got to feed me crunchy peanut butter on a spoon. Brave students gave me a pat on the head. Really brave students touched my tail and tried not to squeal. And then the 3000 took me home to my time and arranged to pick me up the next week to do it all over again.

It turned out that possums are great time travelers. No rashes, memory loss, or upset tummies. My trip back to Twigs's time had proved that, so the 3000 had recruited me to be a living historical exhibit. My job was to help interest the future in the past.

As for what Theodore Wirth Park and the surrounding city looks like ten thousand years from now—I wish I could tell you. It's really something. But they made me agree to a nondisclosure contract that swore me to secrecy. Time contamination, you know.

But maybe it won't get me in too much trouble if I mention that cupcakes are still popular in the future. And one more thing: There's a life-sized statue of a woolly mammoth outside the Theodore Wirth Wildlife and Time Preservation Sanctuary. It's made of bronze and has a possum, raccoon, and chipmunk riding on its back. Please don't mention the chipmunk to the Earl of Sussex. Red squirrels can be awful sensitive about such mistakes as that.

The end

THE BRAVE
ADVENTURERS